Murder Under A Western Moon

A Mona Moon Mystery
Book Eleven

Abigail Keam

Worker Bee Press

Penny Baker Blooper Editing
Author's photograph by Peter Keam
Book cover design by Peter Keam
Special thanks to Melanie Murphy, Jesse Coffey, and Liz Hobson.

ISBN 978 1 953478 14 6
6 20 23

Published in the USA by

Worker Bee Press
P.O. Box 485
Nicholasville, KY 40340

Books By Abigail Keam

The Josiah Reynolds Mysteries

Death By A HoneyBee I
Death By Drowning II
Death By Bridle III
Death By Bourbon IV
Death By Lotto V
Death By Chocolate VI
Death By Haunting VII
Death By Derby VIII
Death By Design IX
Death By Malice X
Death By Drama XI
Death By Stalking XII
Death By Deceit XIII
Death By Magic XIV
Death By Shock XV
Death By Chance XVI
Death By Poison XVII
Death By Greed XVIII
Death By Theft XVIX

The Mona Moon Mystery Series
Murder Under A Blue Moon I
Murder Under A Blood Moon II
Murder Under A Bad Moon III
Murder Under A Silver Moon IV
Murder Under A Wolf Moon V
Murder Under A Black Moon VI
Murder Under A Full Moon VII
Murder Under A New Moon VIII
Murder Under A British Moon IX
Murder Under A Bridal Moon X
Murder Under A Western Moon XI
Murder Under A Honey Moon XII

1

Mona Moon and her new husband, Robert Farley, were halfway up the passenger ship's ramp that would whisk them away to Great Britain where they would spend their honeymoon at the Duchy of Brynelleth, Robert's ancestral home, when a messenger frantically flagged them down. "Miss Maplewood! Miss Maplewood! I've got an urgent telegram for you."

Robert touched Mona's elbow as if to guide her forward. "Leave it, Mona. It's nothing more than a congratulatory telegram on our marriage."

"Only Violet knew which ship we were taking to Great Britain and our assumed names. I must read it. It might be important."

"Anybody could have tracked us down. Let's get on board first."

"Wait, Lord Bob," Mona replied, using her nickname for Robert, who was Duke of Brynelleth. She made her way down the ramp. "Excuse me. Pardon me. So sorry," she said, after bumping into passengers on the ramp going in the opposite direction.

Exasperated, Robert followed. "Mona, we have spent the last five days fending off newspaper men by sneaking to New York. Now I want some alone time with you so I can do things that no one mentions in polite society."

"Well, how rude," gasped one matron passing by.

"So sorry, Madame," apologized a red-faced Robert, tipping the brim of his hat. He ran after Mona. "See what you made me do?"

"I never told you to loudly broadcast our personal lives to the public. I think that esteemed lady might need smelling salts," Mona said, grinning and looking over her shoulder at Robert. She finally reached the dock and yelled while waving her arm, "Here, boy. Here."

"Miss Maplewood?" Maplewood was the assumed name the Farleys were traveling under.

"The one and only." She tipped the courier fifty cents.

After he didn't leave but looked expectantly at her, Mona said, "You may go now."

"I'm sorry, Miss, but the telegram requires an answer. I'm not supposed to leave without it."

"It's Mrs.," Mona replied absentmindedly as she tore open the telegram and read.

POTENTIAL RIOT AT MONTANA MINE STOP DEAD MINER STOP POSSIBLE MURDER STOP COME AT ONCE STOP RUPERT HUNT

"What is it, darling?" Robert asked, noticing Mona's face drain of color.

Mona handed Robert the telegram.

"That's not cricket," Robert said after reading it. "What do you want to do?"

Mona asked the telegram messenger, "Do you have a pencil, young man?"

"Yes, ma'am." The lad handed Mona the pencil tucked in his cap.

Mona scribbled a line on the pad the boy handed to her. "Send this off immediately and tell no one about my reply. Understand?" She gave him a dollar.

He gazed at the silver dollar in surprise. "Thank you, ma'am. I won't tell a soul."

"Get along with you and send that off as soon as you get back to the office."

"To whom do you want this message sent, ma'am?"

"To the sender of this telegram. Hurry and don't lollygag."

The boy tipped his cap and ran off.

"Oh, dear. I forgot to give back his pencil," Mona muttered, realizing it was too late to call him. She didn't want to attract attention and tucked the small pencil in her purse. She turned to face Robert, trying to act nonchalant. "Have the reporters recognized us yet?"

Robert looked about casually, glancing at the knot of reporters and photographers reporting on people of note embarking on the ship to Europe. Well-known passengers were reported in the society columns of the newspapers. "Not yet, but if we linger any longer, they will. The black wig you have on helps, but we need to leave before we are spotted. I see one eyeing us now."

A photographer, chattering to a few of his colleagues, kept glancing at Robert and Mona.

Robert turned away as did Mona. "What do you want to do, my love?"

"Robert, I've got to go to Montana. That's our biggest copper mine. Whatever trouble is brewing there, I've got to put an end to it. Too much is at stake."

Taking a deep dissatisfied breath, Robert hailed a porter and gave him their luggage claim tickets. "Bring them off the boat and onto the dock. I think they are in our stateroom. Please hurry." Robert handed the porter two dollars. "I'll give you three more if you can bring our trunks down in six minutes."

The porter gawked at the two dollars. "Three more dollars?"

Robert nodded.

The porter rushed up the gangplank, pushing passengers out of his way. The usual tip was twenty-five cents.

Hiding his great disappointment that their honeymoon was interrupted, Robert wrapped his arm around Mona, knowing she was let down as well. "It will be all right, darling. We have our entire lives to enjoy our honeymoon."

Mona pressed her hand on Robert's arm. "Oh, Robert. I'm so sorry. Our trip is ruined."

The porter rushed down the ramp with their

trunks just as Robert kissed Mona's hair, causing the wig to shift a bit, exposing her platinum hair.

An alert newspaper reporter, seeing the platinum hair, yelled. "Hey, guys, it's Mona Moon and the Duke of Brynelleth, her new husband!" The group turned and eyed them suspiciously.

Robert grabbed a fist full of dollar coins from his pants pocket and handed them to the porter. "Our plans have changed. Put these trunks in storage. I'll have someone call for them. You will be contacted. What's your name friend?"

"Bill Moses."

Seeing the contingent of reporters now rushing toward them, Robert began pushing Mona along the wharf and toward the cab stand. "Sorry, darling, but we've got to run. No time to wait."

Both Mona and Robert jumped into a cab before anyone could snap a photograph of them. The cabbie merged into a line of cars and was soon lost in the hustle and bustle of New York traffic.

Looking out the back window to see if they were being followed, Mona ordered, "Take us to Penn Station, please."

The cabbie nodded and sped toward the railroad station.

Mona leaned into Robert and wrapped her coat closer around her. "Montana, ready or not. Here we come!"

2

Rupert Hunt met the couple at the Butte, Montana train station. Snow had fallen, and the Moon-Farleys were inadequately dressed for neither the terrain nor climate.

Mona shivered as she stepped off the train. It was a lonely depot crudely made of logs and brick that someone started whitewashing and then quit halfway through, which gave the depot a lackadaisical appearance. Mona looked at the uncomfortable wooden pews and Currier and Ives prints hanging on the walls in the empty waiting room.

Robert followed closely behind, pulling his coat collar tightly up around his neck.

"Mrs. Maplewood, so nice to see you," Rupert said, shaking Mona's hand. He peeked around her. "Where's your luggage?"

"I'm afraid all I have is my makeup case. We were just boarding our ship and had to dash rather quickly after we received your telegram."

"Sorry about the timing, but it couldn't be helped." Rupert led Mona and Robert to his vehicle. It was a battered truck splattered with muddy slush and huge wheels encased in snow chains. The Moon Enterprises logo was emblazoned on the side. "Not very pretty is she, but she's the only thing that goes in this snow without tread wheels."

"What's happened?" Mona asked.

"I'll tell you in the truck. Not here." Glancing at other passengers getting off the train, Rupert helped Mona in the vehicle and then went to the driver's side and got in.

Robert jumped up into the truck next to Mona and slammed the door shut. His socks and shoes were wet from the snow. "This truck is awfully high."

Rupert patted the dashboard. "Yeah, but she's reliable. Need the ground clearance through the snow and mud. That's all I care about."

As the truck moved through Butte, Mona

took stock. It was a dreary-looking town with tall brick smelters which spewed noxious fumes into the air. Everything looked yellow—the buildings, the snow—even the people brave enough to venture on the cornmeal-colored sidewalks. After all, Butte was a mining town, and the smelters were its heart.

"First thing I want to do is get some warm clothes. We got on the train with just the clothes on our backs," Mona said, shoving her hands in her coat pockets. "Can this truck get any warmer?"

"She will but takes a moment or two. The stores are closed now, but we can purchase suitable clothing early tomorrow. I did buy a few things for you both, but Miss Mona, I wasn't sure of the size for you."

Mona answered, "As long as it is warm, I don't care. The wind is really sharp here in Big Sky Country. Cuts right into a person."

Robert blew on his hands before rubbing them. "I'm starving. Where can we get something to eat?"

"Nothing is open in Butte at this hour. We'll go to my house near Moon Mine. I left a stew on the stove and bought bread this morning. One of the miner's wives bakes for me. She made some sweet rolls as well."

"Sounds delightful," Mona said. She was famished as well.

Rupert added, "And I have coffee and whiskey. That will warm you up. I also have eggs and butter, but no milk."

"Can you tell us what happened, Rupert?" Mona was impatient. She hoped to solve this miner problem within a few days and then leave for her honeymoon.

Rupert hit a bump on the road and the entire truck bounced, causing Mona and Robert to hit their heads on the truck roof.

"Sorry about that," apologized Rupert. "The roads are not so good up here. It causes a lot of wear and tear on the vehicles. We go through tires like nobody's business."

"Get on with the tale, my good man," Robert encouraged.

"Who died at the mine and was it really murder?" Mona asked.

"You have over a hundred men working in the mines for a total of sixteen-hour shifts of eight hours each per person. They come from all different parts of the world, and many do not speak proper English. They are rough-hewn characters accustomed to working with their hands and backs. Some came with their families, but most are bachelors—lonely and prone to drink because they are bored. They also bring their prejudices with them."

"Rupert, get to the point," Mona said. "Stop bandying words."

"When they drink, the men argue. Two men got into a fight. It was broken up, but later one of the men was found dead with a knife stuck between his ribs. A Pole by the name of Piotr Wojcik."

"I take it the man Mr. Wojcik fought with was arrested."

"Yes, Mona, and the men are hopping mad and threatening to go on strike."

"Why?"

"The man the sheriff arrested is from the Blackfoot tribe. The other men don't want to work with Indians and want you to quit hiring them."

"You mean to tell me the men want to strike,

even though I pay the highest wages in the mining business?" Mona muttered, somewhat stunned. "I pay them above the national average because I don't want strikes."

"Sounds like a bunch of ungrateful blokes to me," Robert remarked. "Where else could they make that kind of money during the Depression?"

"This isn't about money. It's about hate and mistrust. When a man descends into a mine, he's got to rely on his fellow workers. The trust in each other is simply not there. Of course, the language barrier is a big factor."

Mona said, "I've run into this problem before at Brynelleth with Polish workers and in Mesopotamia with the nomadic tribes. I think I can sort this problem out."

Rupert raised an eyebrow displaying his skepticism. He was not so sure. This wasn't a case of simple contract negotiation, but involved long-held beliefs that were deeply ingrained in the miners. He had seen this type of mistrust in the Great War, but decided to keep his peace—for now. He would let what he said sink in.

The rest of the trip was made in silence. Rupert was tired and struggled to keep the truck on the road. Mona drifted off and rested her head on Robert's shoulder. Even the occasional shuddering of the truck did not rouse her. After forty-five minutes of rough traveling, Rupert suddenly slammed on the brakes. "Here we are, my little Shangri-La."

Mona straightened up. She and Robert looked out the window to see a forlorn-looking, two-story clapboard house with a makeshift porch stacked with firewood. A few black window shutters, blown off by the wind, were scattered haphazardly on the ground, and rainwater barrels strewn near the gutters were filled with frozen water. The house, long ago whitewashed, was peeling, giving it a gloomy, unkempt look.

It was hardly the sort of place Mona wanted to spend time with her new husband. "You live here?"

"Yeah, and you know what's worse—you own the joint."

"I own this?" Stunned, Mona was helped out of the truck by Robert and braced herself.

3

Mona staggered through the snow and sludge until Robert picked her up and carried her to the porch. She shielded her eyes from snow drifting down from the trees surrounding the house.

Rupert pushed open the front door and hurriedly built up the fire in the potbellied stove before he lit the kerosene lamps. "It will warm up in a bit, folks. There's a blanket on the couch. Stay covered until the stove heats up." Rupert lifted the lid from the cast-iron Dutch oven on the top of the potbellied stove. "Ah, the stew has grown cold, but will warm up in a jiffy." He gave the stew a quick stir and started a pot of coffee.

Mona looked about and realized they were standing inside a log cabin with shoddy-looking clapboard sheathing the outside on the logs. She wondered why the subterfuge. The inside of the house was tidy and well-appointed with sturdy, comfortable furniture covered in local indigenous fabrics as well as handcrafted rocking chairs. A staircase led to bedrooms upstairs while dividing the downstairs into a living, dining, and cooking area in one room on the left and a bedroom on the back right. The kitchen consisted of a countertop that spanned the length of the back wall, and shelves, supporting dishes and food goods, were hand-hewn planks of wood. In the middle of the countertop sat the tin farm sink with a hand pump for water. The grey water from the sink was drained into a barrel outside the kitchen window. Nothing was wasted in this house.

Mona's heart sank when she realized the house apparently did not have hot water or even an indoor bathroom. Oh, well, she had endured worse before. She only hoped that the outhouse wasn't too far from the cabin.

Fishing rods, snow shoes, and gun racks lined the walls. A moose head with gigantic antlers loomed over the walled-up fieldstone fireplace where a potbellied stove now resided on its hearth. The stove's exhaust pipe exited out a hole punched through the fireplace exterior. Towers of split firewood in metal boxes shadowed each side of the iron stove. Mona guessed the metal containers were to protect the wood from any sparks that may escape when the stove door was opened.

"Did you install the stove, Rupert?" Mona asked.

"It heats better than the fireplace. Heat would just go up the chimney. I learned the hard way. Almost froze my fanny off during the first snow."

"May I help?" Robert asked, looking about for food. He was starving.

"No, thanks. This will take the edge off, Lord Bob." He put a basket of sweet rolls on the rough plank dining table and opened a window to retrieve a plate holding a slab of butter. Grinning at Mona and Robert, he boasted, "Better than an ice box." He tapped the butter, which was frozen, with a knife. "Better put this on the stove, too." Rupert placed the tin plate on the stove and waited a minute for the butter to soften. Once that was accomplished, he put butter and rolls on the table. "Help yourselves. I'll get more tomor-row."

Robert and Mona made their way to the table and sat down, greedily eying the rolls while Rupert gathered the blanket from the couch and placed it over Mona's shoulders.

"Thank you," she said, wrapping the blanket around her.

Seeing that Mona and Robert were hesitant to eat without him, Rupert tossed some rolls on two plates with large dollops of now soft butter each, placing the plates before them. "Don't wait on me. Go ahead and eat. I need to warm the stew."

With arms akimbo, Rupert studied his small pantry. "Now I know I had a jar of peach preserves somewhere. Hmm. Ah, there it is." Rupert placed a mason jar of preserves with a large spoon near Robert. "Help yourself."

"Please join us," Mona encouraged. "You must be hungry as well."

"One moment." Rupert cracked six eggs and stirred them into the stew. After a moment or two, he brought over the Dutch oven and coffeepot to the table. Lifting the oven's lid, Rupert doled heaping mounds of the stew onto their plates and poured the coffee. "That should do it," he announced proudly. "I always thought I could throw a good meal together without many ingredients."

Robert dove in and announced with a mouthful of buttered bread dipped in the stew juice, "Pretty good, Rupert."

Mona didn't hold back either shoving food onto her spoon. "We are very hungry. There was a six hour wait on the train north of Sheridan, Wyoming. They had to dig the train out of a little snow avalanche landing on the tracks. The train ran out of food except for crackers, so we ate a lot of saltines and drank clam juice. This meal is heaven."

"Sheridan, huh?" Rupert muttered.

"Why? What's the matter?" Mona asked, alarmed at Rupert's tone.

"Maybe the snow on the tracks wasn't due to nature."

"What do you mean, Rupert?"

"There's a secessionist movement growing in that area."

Robert asked, "Who is seceding from what and joining whom, Rupert?"

"It's a group of ranchers and farmers unhappy with what they are receiving in federal aid. They believe President Roosevelt is favoring cities and leaving country folk high and dry because of the area's lack of population. They are getting strong local support. I think an actual organization will emerge from it."

"And their aim is to do what?" Robert asked.

"Create a new state."

"I thought people had learned their lesson about seceding from the Union," Mona said.

Rupert answered, "Oh, it's not about seceding from the United States. It's about taking part of Wyoming and a little bit of Montana to create a whole new state."

Mona perked up. "That might have a negative effect on the mines. Are any of our miners sympathetic?"

"Of course, some are. There is a lot of anti-government sentiment with miners, but I haven't seen any overt action yet even though I'm hearing whispers of it. That's why I've postponed my trips to your other mines. Too much is going on here."

Mona asked, "Does this secessionist movement have anything to do with the killing of the miner?"

Rupert scratched his chin. "Don't know yet. Still looking into it."

Mona, Robert, and Rupert ate in silence until Mona had her fill. "Rupert, what is your job here—undercover I mean."

Rupert wiped his mouth with his shirt sleeve. "I'm a driver."

"You drive the ore to the smelters in Butte?"

"No, I bring supplies in for the store, run errands for Dr. Driscoll. Sort of a gopher, you might say. Whatever needs to be brought in, I bring. It gives me a chance to snoop."

Mona said, "I felt your weekly reports were holding back. Can you be more specific? After all, you sent that telegram urging me to come."

"Haven't given you my full report. I need to be sure about what is going on here. I had only parts of the jigsaw puzzle to give you."

Robert asked, "And now you think you know?"

"Yes, I do. Will give you a full report tomorrow. We're all tired. I need to sleep."

Mona heard a wolf pack howling in the distance. She and Robert glanced at each other. Mona wondered if she had made a mistake in coming, but she was the head of Moon Enterprises and had to see the situation through to its successful conclusion. It was just she thought she'd be wearing one of her new evening gowns and dancing in Robert's arms aboard a luxurious passenger ship heading for England—a passenger ship with hot water, champagne, and a private bath. Mona sighed and closed her eyes for a few seconds, realizing that as so often in the past, she had to make the best of a bad situation.

"You two take that room," Rupert said pointing to the back bedroom with a brass bed. "I'll take the couch, so I can feed the stove. Need to keep it going all night if the house is to be warm in the morning."

"Aren't there bedrooms upstairs?" Mona asked, hoping she and Robert would have some privacy.

"Yeah, but I can't keep the stove burning hot enough to warm the entire house. Keeping the first floor warm is the best I can do. You can sleep up there, but you'll freeze—even with blankets."

"I see," Robert said. "We'll take the bedroom on this floor."

Mona could tell Robert had grown impatient with the situation, and she was concerned about his unhappiness. After all, this was supposed to be his honeymoon as well.

Rupert said, "I would suggest keeping the bedroom door open so the warm air can flow in there."

Robert frowned and started to speak, but thought better of it.

Mona knew what he was thinking. Was Rupert pranking them—deliberately keeping them from enjoying their first weeks together as husband and wife? She decided to intervene. "Come Robert. Let's adjourn. I'm worn out. A good night's sleep will put us both to right."

Rupert offered, "I'll clean up. You guys go on. I'll explain everything in the morning."

"You'd better, Rupert." Mona's voice had an edge to it, and she'd make sure her snub-nosed revolver would be on the nightstand within easy reach. She didn't trust Rupert completely. She had hired him because she thought it took a thief to catch a thief, but Rupert was mischievous. He liked to play games.

Robert closed the bedroom door halfway allowing the heat to reach them without exposing them to any prying eyes. He hung a bell on the door handle that would ring if anyone tried to enter the room as they slept. He had learned this trick from Violet, Mona's maid, and it worked well.

As Mona and Robert didn't have any night clothes, they merely took off their shoes and coats before climbing into the creaky bed which squeaked every time they shifted.

Robert muttered curse words while he tried to find a comfortable position in the sagging bed while Mona giggled at the absurdity of their situation. Robert soon joined her in laughter as they tried to muffle the sounds in their feather pillows. It wasn't long though, before they fell asleep in each other's arms as Robert spooned Mona, holding her close.

Sleeping soundly, they didn't notice a hand slipping around the door and muffling the bell. Rupert quietly stepped inside the room. He went through Mona's purse on the nightstand while leaving the gun alone and then carefully rummaged her makeup case. After searching Mona's belongings, Rupert crept out of her room as silently as a stalking mountain cougar on a hunt.

What Rupert didn't know was that Mona was awakened by a squeaking floorboard and watched him stealthily search her things.

What trick was Rupert playing on her now?

4

Mona awoke the next morning before dawn and lit the kerosene lamp on the nightstand. Making a diligent effort not to awaken Robert, she crept out of bed and slipped on her shoes. The floor was freezing. Fumbling through her carrying case, she pulled out a comb and forced it through her hair before tying it up in a chignon.

Oh, how Mona wished Violet was with her now. Violet would keep her tidy. Violet was supposed to meet them in Paris after they had visited Brynelleth, Robert's ancestral home. Mona now wondered if she and Robert would ever make it there themselves.

Tugging on her traveling suit jacket in an effort to straighten her outfit, Mona looked at the mirror above the dresser and twisted her mouth in disapproval. She muttered, "I haven't looked this bad since I worked in the Zagros Mountains mapping the border between Persia and Iraq."

She went over to Robert. "Are you awake, dear?"

Robert opened one eye. "How cold is it?"

"For someone who grew up in a drafty castle with no central heat and only fireplaces for warmth, this should be a cinch."

"Yes, darling, but how cold is it?" Robert moaned.

"Oh, get up, sleepy head," Mona laughed, yanking the covers off Robert.

Robert reached up and grabbed them back.

"I'm going to make breakfast and get to the bottom of this murder business, so we can get out of here. You can be of great help if you would just get up."

"Righto, Mona. Be there in a second."

Mona went into the living area and looked about for Rupert. He was not to be found, but there was a pan of heated water on the stove. Delighted, Mona carried the pan over to the sink and washed her face. Two new toothbrushes with a tin of tooth powder and clean towels sat on the kitchen counter. After brushing her teeth, Mona felt renewed and set about making breakfast. Gathering the butter plate from outside the window, Mona buttered several pieces of bread she sliced from the loaf left on the counter and threw the pieces into the iron skillet sitting on the potbellied stove. She cracked two eggs and poured them into the holes poked through the bread. Seeing the *bird's nests* were frying up nicely, she put the coffee on the stove to boil.

Rupert noisily threw open the door with an armload of wood and grunted, "Good morning." He stoked up the fire before pouring himself a cup of weak coffee. Looking into the sizzling skillet, he asked, "Has one of those got my name on it?"

Mona nodded, "Sure. They are your bread and eggs."

"No, actually you paid for them."

Mona scooped both bird's nests and put them onto plates.

"Is Lord Bob still asleep?" Rupert asked with derision cutting his food with a knife and fork in the British fashion. He didn't really care for Lawrence Robert Emerton Dagobert Farley,

Duke of Brynelleth, and used every opportunity to mock him.

Mona sighed, "I wish you'd keep a civil tongue in your mouth."

"I've heard you call him *Lord Bob*."

"I'm allowed to. You are not."

"Noted." Rupert ate his eggs and fried bread. He also scooped up some of the sweet rolls left over from last night and lathered peach preserves on them.

"Let His Grace have a moment. He was expecting to be waking up at Brynelleth today, instead of this dump you've brought us to. Why didn't we stay in a hotel in Butte—a hotel with running hot water and a dining room?"

Rupert answered, "Because I wanted to keep your arrival a secret for a day or so."

Mona cut into her egg. The yolk seeped into the fried bread which Mona ate with relish. "The purpose being?"

"Once the swells know you are here, they will whisk you away to their swank homes, hold dinner parties in your honor, lie straight to your face, and then send you on your merry way."

"Lie to me about what?"

"You sent me west to investigate the Moon mines. I've inspected three and this is the worst mine for corruption so far. The other mines are too small to be of any consequence."

Mona perked up. "Go on."

"The very same people who came to your wedding two weeks ago are wholesaling your copper to a competitor, selling off the safety equipment, overcharging miners for goods at your store, and stirring up strife among the miners to create a diversion."

"That's quite a list. Are all the managers in on it?"

"No. Those who object to what's happening are threatened."

Mona asked, "How are they threatened?"

"Mysterious things befall them. A hunting accident. A car accident. A sudden tumble down a staircase. Their families are threatened, too. I've heard rumors of the wives being accosted as a message for their husbands."

"Have any proof?"

"While the swells were gone to your wedding, I found a second set of books in one of the manager's homes. The man is not too clever. It openly lists copper deliveries, dates, and receiver names. He didn't even bother with a cipher."

"Could it be a plant?" Mona asked while eating from a spoon loaded with preserves.

"You wouldn't think so if you met the gentleman, and you will."

Mona got up from the table and poured them both a cup of coffee.

"It's why I had you use the surname of Maplewood and had you hide your hair when you got off the train. I want you to mosey around the camp in disguise and talk to the miners and their families. See what's on their minds. Once you discover the truth, we'll take it from there."

"You said the families won't talk."

"The wives might if they think you are my cousin, Mrs. Maplewood from Alabama, visiting for a couple of days. Just keep your head covered. That white hair is a dead giveaway. You can wear sunglasses to protect you from snow glare. That's a good excuse to hide your yellow eyes."

Mona leaned back in her chair. "I see. What about this miner who was killed?"

"The majority of miners don't like working with the Indians because they think they are heathens. Since the Indian Reorganization Act, many natives have gone back to their tribal practices and have abandoned Christianity they accepted in the Indian schools. Many of the European immigrants are deeply religious and superstitious. They think the Indians are in league with the Devil."

"Is that what started the fight between the miners?"

"Yep, Piotr Wojcik plucked at a medicine bag the Indian was wearing. The Indian objected and a fist fight erupted. It was broken up and the two men went their own ways, but Wojcik was found two hours later stabbed to death."

"The Indian was arrested on what evidence?"

"None. That's what they do here. There is deeply held prejudice against native peoples."

"What do you think?"

Rupert answered, "The Indian may have killed Piotr Wojcik, but I believe the Pole was paid to start a fight, and then was murdered by whoever paid him to create chaos in the mine. It's a classic divide and conquer strategy."

Mona realized the magical trip of which she had dreamed was now a shadow fading fast. Her first impulse was to shed some tears over her disappointment, but she recognized a duty to her company and to the employees who worked for Moon Enterprises. This was a two-step problem. Root out the corruption and discover the true culprit of the murdered Pole, but she had another agenda as well.

She pulled the bell from her pocket and tossed it over to Rupert. Its crystal clear ringing filled the room. "Odd isn't it, how this didn't ring last night when you crept into our room?"

Rupert laid the bell on the table. "Oh."

"Yes, oh. Everything you've told me can easily be a pile of manure. I hope this is not another kidnapping attempt on your part to extort money from me, Rupert, because I will have to really shoot you this time."

Nonchalantly, Rupert picked up his fork and continued eating. "I suppose you're holding your snub nose revolver under the table."

Mona nodded. "Yes, and I checked it this morning. The bullets are still in their chambers, and the gun is pointed right at your nether regions."

Rupert hastily replied, "I can explain."

"Right now would be a good time to start."

Looking like a boy who had been caught stealing peaches from his neighbor's tree, Rupert explained, "I sneaked into your room—well, just to keep my hand in, so to speak."

Mona laughed. "You can do better than that. You used to think fast on your feet."

Blushing, Rupert said, "The impulse to steal is hard to ignore. I've been a good boy for a very long time, and you are very rich. I just wanted something—a memento of sorts."

"You have no idea how bizarre that sounds."

"But coming from Rupert, it sounds about right," said Robert, striding into the room. "What did you nip, you little weasel?"

"A powder compact," Rupert said sheepishly.

Shaking her head, Mona said, "You can keep it, Rupert. I'll get another one today at the store."

Rupert burst out laughing, "You think the company store has facial powder. You have no idea what's happening here. You've focused too much on Mooncrest Farm and Brynelleth, giving the mine managers too much power. Now there's the dickens to pay." He reached into his pocket and tossed the compact on the table. "I don't want it now. You've taken all the fun out of stealing it."

"Please, Mona, sack this miscreant," Robert said. "Or let me ring his neck."

"No, Robert. It takes a thief to understand a thief. Rupert's doing his job."

Robert pantomimed grabbing the little man's neck and throttling him.

Rupert winced.

"Now Rupert, this is what's going to happen. I'm going to verify everything you've said, and then I'll make a move. First things first, I want to speak with this miner's wife who bakes for you."

"We can go this morning, Mona. She knows my cousin is coming and made a buttermilk pie. I'll make some excuse to leave as I know she will have you stay for a cup of coffee over women talk, but you can't go in those clothes. I have some pants and boots that will do the trick. That outfit you have on is too fancy."

"Why didn't you give the clothes to me last night?" Mona asked, exasperated. "Look at me. My hose are torn. My clothes are in shambles due to sleeping in them. My coat is inadequate for the weather."

"Because Rupert loves his little torments, Mona," Robert complained. "I wish you'd fire him."

Mona grinned at Rupert. "I just might, but I want to speak to this wife first."

"May I at least thump him on the head?"

"Maybe later, dear," Mona teased. "Right now Rupert has to take me to meet the sweet woman who has made me a pie."

Rupert shrugged in response to Robert's threat.

Robert asked, "What am I to do while you're gone?"

Mona looked around. "There is a bed to be made and dishes to wash."

"But I'm a duke!"

"At the moment, you're the house wife. Get to it," Mona said, smiling. She always thought Robert's sense of entitlement was something to be curbed.

Robert saluted Mona before pouring a cup of coffee.

Mona quickly changed into the pants and boots that Rupert offered and hurried out to the truck. "Let's go," she said, after climbing in.

Rupert put the truck into first gear and off they went as Mona marveled at the countryside. The road created a brown slash through the stark white powder covering all but the trees. Mona put on her sunglasses as the snow glare proved too much and pulled her cap over her hair which was the same color as the snow. She had never been to this part of the country and was rapidly gaining a newfound esteem for its wild beauty. It was a landscape that demanded respect as it was also a landscape that could kill you.

As always, she carried her snub nose revolver since Mona never knew what to expect with Rupert. After all, he could have made a deal with the corrupt managers and was delivering Mona to her death.

Mona knew she was taking a chance being alone with him.

5

Mona held on to the strap dangling from the truck's roof for dear life as it bumped its way into Mooncrest Village, a small town established for the miners. There was a general store which also acted as a post office. Near the store sat a doctor's office, a block house which offered men's and women's shower facilities complete with toilets and sinks accompanied by wall mirrors, a non-denominational chapel, a laundry facility with two crank washers and clotheslines for drying, a community center, and a small park with benches, tables, and barbeque pits. Encompassing this little oasis of civility was a community of fifty-five two bedroom clapboard houses built for the miners.

Mooncrest Village looked dreary, poor, and

unkempt. No children played outside in the snow. No one gathered about the store. The road had not been cleared of snow and was slushy where it was not icy. The houses showed chipped paint and trash spilled out of cans standing in front as much of it escaped, blowing across the gravel road. There were no sidewalks and the hills behind the houses were dotted with unsightly outhouses.

After she spied a woman exiting an outhouse, Mona exclaimed, "I gave orders that the outhouses were to be torn down after the septic tanks were installed!"

Rupert gave a smug look. "That is one of the many problems with this mine. The septic tanks were not installed properly, and the waste leaked into the water supply. Made people sick, so the outhouses were kept."

"Why weren't the tanks dug up and reinstalled properly?"

"Gee, that's a question for the general manager, Miss Mona."

"What about the community bathing house? It has showers and toilets."

"Broken down. Not fixed yet."

"How do people keep clean?"

Rupert mumbled, "How do they indeed?"

Disturbed, Mona looked out the window. "Why hasn't the trash been picked up? All the trash cans are spilling over."

"Now that's a question you need to ask your general manager, Miss Mona."

"I get it, Rupert. I didn't keep my eye on the ball, but I did pay for modern conveniences and expected the problems with the camp to be addressed. I give orders and expect them to be followed."

"You know Mona, there is an old saying. People do what you inspect, not what you expect."

"But Rupert, you forget one thing. You were sent out here to inspect. You were supposed to be my eyes and ears. You should have let me know about these problems earlier. I can't be in two places at once."

Rupert didn't respond until he pulled in front of a house numbered 32. "Now keep your language simple. No fancy words. Keep your hat on. You are my cousin Mona Maplewood from Huntsville, Alabama. Understand?"

Mona nodded.

"Let's do this. Stay in the truck until I come around. Chivalry is not dead here."

Mona spied a woman peeking out a frosted window as Rupert opened Mona's truck door and helped her down. They walked up a snowy pathway to a stoop where a woman met them at the door. Mona noticed icicles hanging from the roof.

"Please. Please, come in out of the cold," the woman said gesturing. She was wearing a faded print dress over woolen pants, heavy socks, several knitted sweaters, and a kerchief on her head. There was a small dab of flour on her nose and chin. Closing the door, she beckoned to a table with four chairs near the potbellied stove, which seemed the favorite way to heat in this part of the country.

Rupert introduced Mona. "Tessie, this is my cousin, Mona Maplewood, from Huntsville, Alabama."

"Howdy-do," replied Tessie, who grabbed Mona's hand in a warm embrace. Her shiny brown eyes studied Mona's face.

"So nice to meet you," Mona said, in her best version of a Southern accent.

"Oh, my dear. Your hands are frozen. Come closer to the stove. It will heat you right up."

Mona liked Tessie's friendliness and outpouring of warmth to a stranger. "Thank you. The heater in the truck barely works." Mona took a seat near the stove, rubbing her cold hands.

"Honey, you take off your hat and glasses."

"I'm still frozen if you don't mind, and my eyes are not used to the snow glare, so I'll keep my glasses on. I hope you don't mind. I'm afraid I didn't prepare for this weather. In Alabama, it's still rather balmy."

"That's quite all right. We let the fire go out at night, and then I stoke it up in the morning. You'd be warmer if you layered up. Look at me. I know I look ridiculous but I stay warm, and we use less wood during the day."

Rupert assured Tessie, "We are going to the store after our visit. We'll get more clothes for Mona then."

Tessie made a face. "That place! You call that a store for the miners. It's more of a robber's den."

"Excuse me?" Mona said.

Tessie looked at Mona's stricken face and

gave a short laugh. "Oh, I'm sorry. Rupert must not have told you what is going on around here. You came to visit. Not hear our tales of woe." Tessie wiped her hands on her apron. "Please stay for a few. I would love to hear of the outside world. A cup of coffee and a raisin muffin to tempt you?"

"That would be nice, Tessie. Yes, thank you," Rupert said, unwrapping a scarf from around his neck.

As Tessie gathered tin plates and food, Mona looked about. The furniture looked rather shabby but the house was clean and tidy. A picture of Jesus hung on the wall near the door as the only art in the room. Similar to the house Mona stayed in last night, the living and dining area plus the kitchen were one large room. The bedrooms must be behind the doors dotting the east wall. Light streamed into the room giving a cheerful ambiance, but most of the windows were still covered with hoarfrost.

"How long have you been here, Tessie?" Mona asked.

Tessie stopped to think, plucking a wisp of stray hair behind her ear. "It's going on two years now. We came right before that Moon witch took over the company."

"A woman runs the company?" Mona asked offhandedly.

Tessie put a plate of one muffin before Rupert and Mona each. "Let me get your coffee."

Rupert teased, "Yes. A woman named Mona Moon owns this mine and several others. Her first name is the same as yours. Isn't that a coincidence?"

"Yes, isn't it," Mona replied, staring down Rupert.

Tessie set cups on the table and sat opposite Mona. "I'm sorry, but I don't have any milk or sugar to offer for your coffee. I used it all up baking this morning."

"Aren't you having a muffin, Tessie?" Rupert asked.

"No. No. I had one this morning. You two go ahead."

"Nonsense." Rupert tore his muffin in half and placed it before Tessie. "Eat."

Tessie smiled and swooped up the muffin half, taking a polite bite. "Your cousin is always ordering me about."

Mona raised an eyebrow. "Does he now? Don't let Rupert bully you, Tessie. He can be terrible."

Tessie took a sip of her coffee and placed her elbows on the table holding the cup. "Don't be hard on Rupert. He's been such a dear to the women of the village since coming here. He buys baked goods from me, his washing done by Mrs. McArthur, his dinner cooked by Mrs. Moore, and his house cleaned by Mrs. Tuttle. I know for a fact if a family is having a difficult time, Rupert will leave a few coins on their stoop."

"Now Tessie, that is supposed to be a secret. No one is to know," Rupert objected.

Mona cocked her head. "I've read of this Mona Moon in both the society and business newspaper columns. She boasts that she pays the highest wages in the country for miners."

"Oh, she does," Tessie said, nodding, "but then the cost of living here . . ." Tessie's voice trailed off.

Rupert spoke up. "The cost of wood and coal for winter, groceries, and incidentals takes most of the miners' pay in the winter."

"Would it be cheaper living in the next town

instead of near the mine?" Mona asked.

"Yes, but the roads are so poorly maintained in the winter, it would be hard for our husbands to get to work on time. Most of us don't have cars."

Mona suggested, "Surely the mine would provide transportation."

Tessie and Rupert guffawed at Mona's suggestion.

Tessie complained, "We were made a lot of promises by Moon Enterprises—good wages, suitable housing, and benefits. Look around, Mona, does this look like suitable housing to you? No proper stove. I bake in a Dutch oven on top of this potbellied stove like every other woman here. Electricity is a no-show. No indoor plumbing. No social activities. Sometimes I cry at the loneliness."

Mona didn't react to Tessie's grievances, but she was alarmed. "Have you always lived in Montana?"

"My husband and I are from Oklahoma. We were sharecropping when the drought started. Then the dust clouds came. Blew all the topsoil off, and the livestock died from starvation. The land was barren. It was horrible. We were down to our last thirty dollars when my husband saw the newspaper advertisement asking for strong men to work in the copper mines, so we thought we'd try our hand at it. We hitched-hiked across the country until we got here. I still have fifteen dollars of that original thirty left but we've not saved a dime since being here. It's paycheck to paycheck in the cold months as the store takes what we've saved in the warm months. Without my baking to fill in the gaps, I don't know what we'd do." Tessie paused for a moment putting her fingers to her mouth as though remembering better times. "Back home, I worked as a secretary for a local church three days a week. Handled their books, ordered purchases like Bibles and hymnals, made bank deposits—that sort of thing. I went to business school after high school for six months. Learned typing, filing, some bookkeeping, and a little bit of shorthand." Tessie looked wistfully away and murmured, "Too much time on my hands here. I want to go home. Really, I do."

Alarmed, Mona reached for Tessie's hand. "I'm so sorry. I had no idea."

Tessie smiled bravely. "Well, honey, it's not your fault."

Rupert snorted in derision.

Mona narrowed her eyes while shooting Rupert a hard look.

"Eat up. Please," Tessie encouraged. "Tell me about the outside world. We get no magazines here. No newspapers. There's a library in the next town, but we never go in the winter, so I haven't any books to read."

Mona regaled Tessie about the latest fashions from Paris and tales of movie stars from Hollywood, but she left out news about European politics as it was too disconcerting. Mona wanted to keep the conversation light.

Tessie said, "I'd love to see a moving picture. I think the last talkie I saw was Jean Harlow in *Red-Headed Woman*. I thought it was rather scandalous, but I liked it."

"I think Jean Harlow is overrated on her looks. I don't think she's pretty at all," Rupert said, digging at Mona since she could have been Jean Harlow's doppelganger. People often remarked on their similar appearance. "Don't you agree, Mona?"

Mona wrinkled her nose at Rupert. "I think Jean Harlow's a doll."

Tessie said, laughing, "I agree. You're the one man I know who doesn't think Jean Harlow is tremendous. My husband has a big crush on her. I think he'd trade me for her if he had a chance."

"I doubt it, Tessie. Your husband adores you. Everyone sees that." Rupert took a last sip of coffee. "Thanks for the cup of Joe, Tessie, but we have shopping to do."

Tessie jumped up from her chair. "Rupert, I've made you a nice sourdough round. You don't slice it. Just tear it apart. And a buttermilk pie for you to take." Tessie proudly displayed her baked goods.

Rupert pointed to a small cake on the table. "Is that for us, too?"

Tessie said, "That is a saffron cake for the tommyknockers."

"The tommy what?" Mona asked, curious.

"Miners take the saffron milk cake for the tommyknockers. You know—mischievous spirits who bedevil the miners. A sort of offering. I know it's a silly superstition, but who knows? Right, Mona?"

Mona patted Tessie on the shoulder. "Whatever satisfies the gods, Tessie. Has there been trouble at the mines?"

Tessie nodded. "Broken equipment mostly and bad lighting in the mines causing the miners to get hurt. Someone keeps breaking the light bulbs. They've gone back to using pitch torches in some areas of the mine. Some think it's deliberate sabotage, but there's been no sign of the black cat."

Mona was confused. "What does a black cat have to do with equipment failure?"

Tessie answered, "That's the sign the IWW uses to signal they're responsible for sabotage."

Rupert asked, "Is there still talk of striking?"

"Murmurs of it as the men are getting spooked, especially with Piotr Wojcik getting killed. It has set the miners' teeth on edge."

Rupert slowly munched on his muffin and took a sip of his coffee. "Think they got the right man for the killing?"

Tessie looked thoughtful. "I don't know. It will be interesting to see what the trial brings out."

Mona said, "I understand a Blackfoot was

arrested for Wojcik's murder. Do you think he'll get a fair trial?"

Tessie rubbed her finger around the rim of her battered tin cup. "I hope so. That Indian bought bread from time to time. He was a quiet man and wouldn't chit chat with me. Just told me what he wanted, gave me a few coins, and left. I never could figure him out."

Rupert added, "I think he and his people are traumatized."

Tessie seemed to take offense. "I think we are all traumatized. Between the dust bowl, the banks failing, the depression, and people fleeing Europe and coming here, you can see despair in every-one's faces. My husband and I thought we had found a safe haven here, but it seems this Mona Moon has turned her back on us. She's no different from the rest of the swells, I guess."

Mona casually asked, "What do others think about this killing?"

"My husband thinks it was murder, but he's not so sure this Indian did the killing."

"Why is that?" Mona asked.

"He won't say, but everyone knows this Wojcik was a bully. My husband says he probably had it coming."

Tired of the conversation, Rupert took a last sip of his coffee and laid two dollars on the table.

Tessie protested, "That's too much!"

"Not if you include the muffins and the coffee. You're not running a charitable house here, Tessie."

"No. NO! I don't want to be paid for the muffins and coffee. Anyone coming into this house is welcomed to my hospitality."

Understanding Tessie's reluctance about the muffins and coffee, Mona laid fifty cents down and picked up one of the dollar bills. "Is this more like it, Tessie?"

The woman smiled. "Yes. Rupert always overpays. Causes me quite a stir."

Rupert gathered the bread and pie. "I'll bring back the pie pan when finished."

"You do that, Rupert." Tessie grabbed Mona's hand. "Please come back to see me before you leave. I'd like you to meet my husband, and it's so nice to talk to someone fresh and new."

Mona patted Tessie's hand. "You can count on it, Miss Tessie. Next time I'll bring my husband as well."

Blushing, Tessie said, "Oh goodness, imagine

someone calling me Miss Tessie. Such Southern manners."

Mona and Rupert gave a last smile and hurried to the truck. He helped Mona in and then handed her the baked goods. Shutting the truck door, Rupert hurried to the driver's side and climbed in.

"Well, what did you think?" Rupert asked.

"Very convincing but I'd like to talk with others. Tessie may be a plant."

"I've taught you very well, Mona. Never trust anyone."

"Life has taught me to be that way, Rupert. Not you. Remember I have worked in some of the most dangerous and isolated parts of the world."

"So be it." Rupert stepped on the clutch and put the truck in first gear. The truck lurched forward, and slowly the two made their way to the general store.

6

Mona and Rupert shook the snow off their boots before stomping into the Mooncrest Village Mining Store. At first glance around, Mona was impressed. It looked like a well-stocked, clean store with notions and sundries on one side and groceries on the other.

A man with a handlebar mustache stood behind the checkout counter while a young lad stocked the shelves. He was a large man with a ruddy face and red hair. It was obvious the man was a descendant from Viking blood. "A good day to you, Rupert. Not working today?"

"I'm taking today off as my cousin came to visit."

Glancing at Mona, Otto protested, "In this weather? She should come in the spring when it's pretty."

"But here she stands before you, Otto, in need of winter clothing. I guess I didn't prepare her for the cold."

"Well, bless my buttons. What a sweet, little thing," Otto said, leering. He twirled one end of his mustache in greeting while his breath was hot in Mona's face.

As she was used to men staring at her, Mona held out her hand. "So nice to meet you, Mr. Otto. I am Mrs. Mona Maplewood." She emphasized the word *Mrs.*

"She's from Huntsville, Alabama," Rupert said.

"That explains the accent. Welcome, little sparrow." He leaned on his meaty hands at the counter. "What can I do you for?"

"I need a better coat." Mona pointed at the thin cloth coat she was wearing. "Another pair of warm pants, a bar of soap—something that smells nice, two flannel shirts . . ."

Otto cut in. "We only have men's shirts."

"That will do. Two pairs of gloves—one pair my size and one extra large in men's wear plus four pairs of wool socks, two men's flannel shirts in ex-large and one pair of pants—large."

"That's a lot of clothes."

"My husband is with me."

Otto glanced out the window. "Where's he now?"

"We left him complaining about the weather at my house. He's a tenderfoot," Rupert explained.

Mona lied, "I'm sorry, but it's true. My husband is a bit of a baby when it comes to cold weather. We had to attend a conference in northwestern Kansas, so we thought since we were out this far from home to continue onward to see Rupert. I had no idea how big this country was or how fierce the weather might be."

Otto asked, "What kind of conference?"

"My husband sells farm equipment, but he's never farmed a day in his life," Mona answered, chuckling.

Both Rupert and Otto chortled as well.

"You'll both need long johns. Nights get cold." Otto pulled out some gloves from a box and laid them on the counter.

"So I've noticed. Can you fill my order?"

"Certainly. Take a seat in the rocking chairs. This might take a minute. There's hot coffee on the stove. Help yourself." Otto began filling Mona's order.

Rupert picked two cups from off the stove and handed one to Mona.

Since the cups didn't look especially clean, Mona declined the coffee and moseyed about the store. There were basic hygiene items—brushes, tooth powder, cloth diapers, lye soap, talc body powder, shaving soap and mugs, shaving brushes, straight razors, rose water, lotions for rashes, tonics for stomach ailments, aspirin, and back pain pills. She also noticed needles and black and white spools of thread, but no patterns or bolts of cloth. There were ready-made dresses, aprons, and children's clothing hanging by the front double door.

There was very little for the women of the village—no lipstick, no face powder, no perfume, no stockings, no pretty shawls, no soft night-gowns—things that give a woman pleasure. No sweets except for rock candy. In other words— no chocolate. No magazines. No newspapers. No books. No underclothing except for long johns. There were lots of knives, hammers, nails, saws, leather aprons and gloves, sawbucks, and other *toys* for men. Mona spied a couple of checker-boards, but no other entertainment and no toys for children except for glass marbles.

"Mr. Otto."

"Just Otto, ma'am. Otto's my first name."

"Pardon me, but I've noticed the dresses by the front door. They look hand-stitched but I see no patterns about."

"Some of the women here are good seam-stresses. They use their own patterns as we don't carry them."

"Where do they get the cloth?"

"From the town over the mountain between here and Butte, which they visit in the summer-time. The roads are cleared starting in May for cars. Sometimes in late April if the weather cooperates. Otherwise, people have to use trucks with tire chains to use the road. Doesn't matter though. Most of the folks around here don't have cars."

"I see." Mona walked a few steps before asking. "I don't see prices on things."

"Prices go up and down depending on de-mand."

Mona resisted the impulse to make a disapproving face. She had established the store to provide the needs of the miners with goods sold at cost. No profit was to be made at the expense of the miners and their families. She said, "Of course. Thank you."

She went over to the grocery side and peered at the bushels of potatoes and apples, baskets of eggs, bunches of carrots, and rutabagas. "You sell meat here?"

"We have an ice house in the back. We store up on ice in the winter to keep summer food from spoiling. Things are different here, ma'am. No fancy refrigerators. When hunters go out, they might bring us a deer or elk."

"No beef or chicken?"

"Chickens are local, but we don't kill them until the hens lay barren. Folks need the eggs more, you see. As for beef, some cows are harvested in the fall when the cattle are sold to eastern markets, but the meat doesn't last long. Everyone in the village buys the beef and cooks it. The men are always hungry for meat."

Mona shrugged. "I just thought since this is big cattle country, beef would be available all year long. Just wondering."

Rupert caught Otto casting a suspicious glance at Mona and was about to intercede when a Blackfoot man and his wife entered the store.

Otto looked up and his pleasant expression turned harsh. "Hey, you two. You know you're not supposed to be in here."

The man replied, "Our contract with Moon Enterprises says that we may shop at the general store."

"Well, I say you are not shopping here."

"But we need food," the woman complained.

"I don't care. Go to the store in the next town. They'll take money from your kind."

"That is twelve miles from here and we are hungry. It is our right to buy at this store," the Blackfoot man said. "We need flour, sugar, and coffee. We want eggs."

Otto grabbed a broom and rushed from behind the counter. "I said git! Go back to your reservation," he said, raising the broom handle.

The woman gasped and put up her arm to ward off an expected blow.

Rupert jumped up and placed himself between the Blackfoot man and Otto. Holding up his hands, Rupert cautioned, "If you hit this miner, he will go to the authorities and will bring attention to the mine. Do you think your boss will like that? Especially after what happened with Wojcik? Use your head, man."

"Our man did not kill Piotr Wojcik," the Blackfoot man insisted. "It was a setup."

"Says who?" Otto spat out. "You?"

The woman tugged on her husband's arm. "Let's go. No help here." Her husband relented and they went outside.

Mona peeked out the window and saw them standing on the porch discussing what to do.

"Sorry you had to see that," Otto said, wrapping up Mona's packages. "Those heathens think they have the same rights as the rest of the miners."

Mona thought it wise not to mention that the federal government thought the Indians did have the same rights as other citizens since June with the Reorganization Act voted into law. Obviously, others thought differently. She remained quiet inwardly seething. She hated bullies.

"Good man," Rupert said, calming the storekeeper. "Let me pay and get out of here, Otto. Mona has an appointment with the doctor."

Otto shot a look at Mona. "Hope you're not ill, ma'am."

Surprised at Rupert's announcement, Mona followed his lead and merely replied, "Just an upset stomach. Nothing serious." She opened her purse. "How much, please?"

"Eighty dollars."

"WHAT!" Mona exclaimed. That was a month's pay for a lot of people.

"Like I said, price depends upon demand."

"I have only fifty dollars to my name until I reach a bank." She turned to Rupert.

"Pay him forty dollars, Mona. I'll take care of the rest. You're my guest." He turned to Otto. "Can you put the rest on my tab, and I'll pay it off at the end of the month?"

"Sure, Rupert. Your account is good with me."

Mona begrudgingly handed Otto two twenty-dollar bills after Rupert signed the store ledger for his account. She could see from the ledger that Rupert owed the store one hundred and seventy-five dollars total.

Otto handed Mona the clothes wrapped in brown paper and tied with string. It was all Mona could do not to declare her real identity and fire the man on the spot.

Rupert took the packages and grabbed Mona's elbow. "Let's go, Cuz."

"Nice to have met you, Otto," Mona said over her shoulder, the words causing her throat to close a bit.

"Hope to see you again, Mrs. Maplewood," Otto said, looking rather smug.

"Not if I can help it," Mona muttered under her breath. Besides bullies, Mona hated cheats.

Rupert threw the packages behind the truck seats. Once he got the truck started, he turned it around and drove away from the village.

"I thought I was supposed to go to the doctor," Mona mused.

"Something we need to do first." Rupert shifted gears and drove until he spied the Native American couple walking down the icy road. Slowing down, he honked his horn.

The couple turned around.

"Roll down your window, Mona." He pulled up to the couple and stopped.

They stared at Mona and Rupert with fearful loathing.

Rupert leaned over and yelled. "Can take you a couple of miles before we have to turn back. My cousin has to see the doctor."

The man and woman exchanged glances. They were tempted to take the ride as it was so cold.

Seeing their indecision, Mona handed the buttermilk pie and bread out the window. "We saw what transpired in the store. Please take these baked goods. They'll ease the burn on the belly."

The woman grabbed the pie pan and bread loaf, giving Mona a sour smile. The Blackfoot man said, "My name is Bill Wheedle. This is my wife, Jess. We live a mile ahead near the creek. We would be obliged if you could take us that far. My wife is tired from the walk."

Rupert thumbed to the back of the truck. "Get in. We'll take you."

The couple climbed into the back, and the man pounded on the truck cab to signal that they were settled.

Rupert drove slowly as not to jostle the couple around the bend and down the mountain.

The man pounded again and Rupert stopped the vehicle.

Seeing the couple had climbed out and were walking toward a makeshift bridge across a running stream, Rupert honked his horn and turned around on the icy road.

Mona looked at the ramshackle shack the couple was heading to and shifted uncomfortably in her seat. These people worked for her and, as such, were under her protection. She was embarrassed and ashamed.

Mona needed to fix the things at Mooncrest Village and the mine.

7

"What seems to be the problem?" the doctor asked. He was young with a sliver of unkempt brown hair falling across his forehead. He was freshly shaven, and Mona caught a wisp of his cologne.

"Upset stomach mostly."

"Try a bit of bicarbonate or a peppermint," the doctor replied, looking distracted. He didn't seem very interested in her medical problem.

"Doctor, is something wrong?" Mona asked. She followed his gaze out the window.

The doctor turned and looked at Mona. "I'm sorry. Let's check you out."

"Should I disrobe?"

"Please don't. The room is so cold. Just lie on the table."

Mona did as instructed.

The doctor rubbed his hands to warm them. "Does it hurt here?" he asked, pressing on her stomach.

"No, sir." Mona could smell a mixture of spearmint and tobacco on the doctor's breath.

The doctor asked again. "Here?"

Mona shook her head.

The doctor helped her to sit up again. "I feel nothing amiss. No bulges, swelling, or knots. Any chance you could be pregnant, Mrs. Maplewood?"

"I don't think so."

"Have you had relations with your husband in the last month?"

"Yes."

"Then you could be pregnant. However, we have no way of testing for pregnancy in this backwoods place. You say you are visiting your cousin, Rupert Hunt?"

"Yes, my husband and I are from Alabama."

The doctor uttered a disgusted sigh. "I would suggest you get tested once you get home. Let's check the rest of you out. Open your mouth please and say ahh."

"Ahhhhhhhhhh."

"Close your mouth please. Have you had your diphtheria vaccination?"

"Yes, sir."

The doctor checked Mona's ears and listened to her heart. "Would you please take off your sunglasses, Mrs. Maplewood? I want to take a gander at your eyes."

"Must I? It is so bright. The light reflecting off the snow hurts my eyes."

"I may not be able to do much in this backwater camp, but I can at least give you a complete physical exam. I need to check your eyes."

Mona slowly took off her dark sunglasses and looked directly at the doctor who seemed astonished at her amber-colored eyes. Only five percent of the world's population had yellow eyes, and the doctor had never seen such eyes before.

Regaining his composure, the doctor had Mona follow the movement of his fingers and check the color of her sclera, pulling on her eyelids. "Look up. Look down. Look to the side, please. Other side, please. Thank you." The doctor stood upright from bending slightly over and looked at

Mona curiously. "Your eyes seem fine. You can put your glasses back on."

Mona put on her sunglasses.

"I've heard of yellow eyes, but never have seen them personally. Very unusual. Let's check your hands and feet. Please take off your gloves and socks."

Mona did as bidden.

The doctor stared at her hands and feet a few seconds before checking them for cuts and discoloration. "Put your gloves and socks back on, please."

"Thank you, doctor."

The doctor studied Mona before launching into a tirade. "Who are you, lady?"

"I'm Mrs. Maplewood from Alabama."

"Okay, then what are you?"

"I don't understand."

The doctor grumbled, "You come in here with a complaint of an upset stomach. There is nothing wrong that I can tell. You seem in perfect health but you are unlike anyone I've met. Your dental work is first rate. It looks expensive with fillings made from gold, and there is a lack of tartar which means you've had your teeth professionally cleaned recently. Then there's the question of your hands and feet. Your hands bear witness to old calluses which meant you once did heavy labor but not anymore. Your heels are hardened as though you have walked great distances. Yet both hands and feet bear an expensive manicure and pedicure. Since the Depression hit, I haven't seen any woman with a manicure or pedicure unless she was on the silver screen starring in the movies. Who are you?"

"I'd like to know why you seem upset, Doctor . . ." She looked at his credentials, hanging on the wall. "Doctor Driscoll. I see that you graduated from Johns Hopkins Medical School."

The doctor blustered, "The fact that you recognize the name of Johns Hopkins tells me that you are an educated woman. Now who the hell are you really?"

"I am a woman seeking answers."

"Why come to me? I'm leaving this godforsaken place soon."

"You are? Why?" Mona jumped off the examination table.

"I came in hopes of doing good, but I am met with nothing but resistance. I can't even treat my patients correctly. As soon as the snow breaks, I'm out of here. I look at the sky every day and pray—no snow, no more snow."

Mona asked, "Don't these people need you? I thought the Moon Enterprises was to provide medical care for the miners and their families."

"Yes, these people need me, but I can't help them. Now, no more questions. I've said enough. It's best you be going."

"Doctor Driscoll!"

"Madam, please leave." The doctor stormed out of the examination room leaving Mona alone.

That was fine with Mona as it gave her time to snoop—and snoop she did.

8

Mona wasn't quite sure what a well-appointed frontier medical facility should look like, but from her experience, this one seemed bare with only a desk, primitive examination table, telephone, and a sturdy light. She opened a door leading to another room where medical emergencies took place. It was well appointed with supplies, equipment, and medical lights needed to operate. She flipped on a light switch. The lights worked so the doctor's office had electricity.

The medical building was similar to a shotgun house with one room opening to another with a main hallway from the front to the back of the house. Mona simply followed the succession of doors. Going through another door, Mona stepped into a recovery room where a man lay in a bed reading. There were ten beds in the room—all of them empty except for his bed. "Oh, I'm sorry. I didn't mean to disturb you."

The man jerked in surprise at seeing a woman enter the room. He pulled a sheet up to his neck. He grinned, saying, "It's been a while since I've seen a woman and a pretty one at that."

Mona answered, "You must not be too sick if you can flatter shamelessly like that."

The patient pulled the sheet from his feet and showed off his cast. "Broke my leg."

"So sorry. How did it happen?"

He confessed, "An accident in the mine. My fault really."

"Oh, too bad," Mona commiserated.

"Look, would you mind handing me another blanket? It's getting cold in here."

Mona looked about and saw blankets stacked on a shelf. She grabbed two and spread them on the patient. Then she threw a lump of coal into the potbellied stove and stoked the fire. "That should make the room warmer."

"It will. Thank you."

Mona brushed the coal dust from her hands and made ready to leave.

The man sat up leaning on his elbows and asked, "Can you stay a minute? It gets lonely here."

The man seemed in earnest, so Mona pulled up a wooden chair next to his bed. "Been here long?"

"A couple of days. The doc wants me to stay for a while so he can keep an eye on me. I live in the bachelor section of the village with two roommates. They can get rough. Might jostle me too much with their horseplay."

"I see." She studied the young man with the slight German accent. He was blond with blue eyes, unshaven, but possessed a good-natured grin that showed a crop of crooked but strong-looking teeth.

She asked, "Are you receiving good care here? I haven't seen any nurses."

"The last nurse left before the first snow. We can't keep them."

"Why is that?"

The man replied, "I'm not sure. You need to ask the doc."

"Is Driscoll a good doctor?"

The young man's face brightened. "The best.

Very dedicated. Hey, my name is Karl Steiner." He struck out his hand.

Mona laughed and shook it. "My name is Mrs. Mona Maplewood. You must be from Germany."

"How can you tell?" Steiner teased. "Did my accent give me away?"

"Just a bit. You speak English remarkably well."

"Thank you. I studied in England for a year, but left when I ran out of money. I followed your American Horace Greeley's advice to 'go west, young man.' Came to America to seek my fortune."

"My, that is going a bit back in history. How has Greeley's advice worked out for you?"

Steiner made a face, pointing to his busted leg. "Not so good."

Mona changed the subject. "What did you study in England, Mr. Steiner?"

Complaining bitterly, Steiner said, "Philosophy. Totally useless in the modern world, I know. Men of the mind have no place in society. It's men of action that the world favors. Philosophy certainly has no place in today's Germany unless it is Nietzsche."

Mona said, "I've read *Thus Spoke Zarathustra*. Found it very interesting. I can't say the same for Mr. Nietzsche's views on women."

"You don't think women should sacrifice themselves for men?" Steiner asked.

Mona said, "I guess you can say I'm an independent thinker like Nietzsche. I think women should have their own opinions, money, and freedom, independent of men."

Steiner said, "You are a modern freethinker indeed, Mrs. Maplewood. Very radical to think women can act on their own volition. You must be an admirer of Eleanor Roosevelt then."

"I am." Mona detected a book peeking out from the sheets. "I see you have a book. What are you reading now?"

Steiner hid the book's title with his hand. "Just some dry political theory. I'm trying to understand what's happening in Europe."

Mona noticed the author was Emma Goldman, the anarchist. "Are you reading *The Place of the Individual in Society* by Goldman?"

Steiner blushed. "I try to be discreet because Dr. Driscoll disapproves of my reading it. Are you a devotee of Miss Goldman?"

"I agree with her that women should be afforded the same opportunities as men, but I think we part company there. I think society needs laws or else we will live with a *might makes right* mentality."

One of the doors to the ward swung open and in stepped Dr. Driscoll, who showed surprise at seeing Mona talking to Karl Steiner. "There you are, Mrs. Maplewood. Your cousin is anxious to take you home. We've been looking for you."

"I lost my way and discovered Herr Steiner all alone and cold."

Steiner said, "Mrs. Maplewood is an angel who saved me from freezing."

"Is that so?" the doctor remarked coldly.

"Doc, Mrs. Maplewood has read *Thus Spoke Zarathustra.*"

Driscoll cocked his head to one side, saying, "Really? Imagine that. Not many women have read that book, let alone know who Nietzsche is."

Mona replied, "More women than you think, Doctor. Perhaps you have never asked women what they have read."

Steiner said, "Touché, Mrs. Maplewood. The doc seems to think all women read are movie magazines, cookbooks, and romance novels, if they can read at all, that is," Steiner said, chortling. "Mrs. Maplewood, I don't know how long you are visiting, but if you have time, please come again. It's nice to talk with someone intelligent."

"Gee, thanks, Karl," Driscoll said.

"No slight on you, Doc, but Mrs. Maplewood is prettier." Steiner gave Mona a bright smile.

The doctor said, "There I can agree with you wholeheartedly."

Rupert Hunt stuck his head inside the door. "There you are, Mona. You disappeared on us. Come, now. We need to get back."

Mona said, "Mr. Steiner, this is my cousin, Mr. Hunt."

"We've met," Steiner said, frostily.

"Hi, Karl. So sorry to see you busted up," Rupert replied.

"I'll mend."

"Nice to have met you, Mr. Steiner."

"Same here, Mrs. Maplewood." Steiner waved goodbye.

"Doctor," Mona said, nodding to Driscoll. "Thank you for your help."

The doctor replied frostily, "Mrs. Maplewood."

Mona left with Rupert and pulled her coat tighter around her to counter the blast of cold air that hit her when opening the front door. They both rushed to the truck and got in as fast as possible. Luckily, Rupert had left the truck running so it was warm or, at least, warmer than the outside air.

"What did you find out?" Rupert asked.

"The facility could use a little improvement, but seems satisfactory. It was Driscoll who was interesting. He said he was leaving as soon as the snow thawed. Rupert, I swear the man seemed fearful, but of what, I don't know."

"I picked that up from the man myself. I wanted to see if you felt it, too."

Mona asked, "If Dr. Driscoll wants to leave, why does he say he has to wait until the snow thaws? You get around okay in your truck."

"I honestly don't know," Rupert replied.

"Do you have much contact with the doctor?"

"Play chess with him now and then. Can't get much out of him, but the doc always appears to be unhappy."

"He wouldn't confide in me either, but then why would he? Let's get back to Robert. I have a job for him."

Rupert turned the truck around and they headed home.

On the way, Mona thought about the strange day.

Something was not right in Mooncrest Village, and she was going to root out the cause. Come hell or high water.

9

"By thunder, where have you been?" bellowed Robert as Mona walked in the door, carrying packages.

Mona hid a grin at seeing Robert in an apron. "All over the place," she answered looking about Rupert's abode. "Robert, you've been busy. Everything looks shipshape."

A stew was simmering on the stove, the table set, the bed made, the floors swept, and the furniture dusted.

Rupert came in with an armload of firewood. "Goodness, what has happened? Mrs. Tuttle won't have anything to do."

"I was stuck here, so I did a little housework to pass the time," Robert answered. "Again, where have you two been?"

Mona took off her coat, scarf, gloves, and hat, throwing them on the back of a chair. She sat down and pulled off her boots.

Robert picked up the packages. "What's this?"

"Warm clothes for you—shirts, socks, pair of pants, and gloves. I want you to go into town tomorrow and send a telegram for me."

Stirring up the stove fire, Rupert turned and said, "Better make it several towns over. The telegraph man in the next town is paid by Moon Enterprises to report any suspicious telegrams."

"How astute of me," Mona said, amused at the irony of the situation. "I'm hoisted by my own petard."

Rupert said, "All the mines pay the telegram man for information. Everyone knows everyone's business."

"I'll go several towns away," Robert answered, glad that he had something to do besides washing dishes.

"Where did you send your telegram to us from, Rupert?"

"I went to Sheridan, Wyoming. Took me two days of traveling."

"Well, that's out of the question. I'm not leaving Mona that long," Robert explained, looking at his wife. "What's your message?"

"I want you to tell Dexter Deatherage to come here immediately. Fly if he has to, and he must bring twenty Pinkertons with him. I think there is something rather rotten going on here. I don't know if the head honchos are merely stealing or setting me up for a fall."

"What kind of fall?" Robert asked, his brows knitted. He turned to Rupert with his fists clenched. "You got us out here. We should be on our way to Europe. What's your conclusion?"

"It could be either. When I've searched the managers' offices, I can't find anything to suggest something nefarious except for a little embezzlement and misappropriation of funds, but I'm convinced something more serious is going on."

"Really?" Mona said, looking askance at Rupert. "You don't think cheating the miners, starving them, being downright hateful to Indians, and a murder nefarious?"

"That's just regular humans being abhorrent to each other. There's nothing new in that." Rupert shrugged. "It is what it is, Mona. How do you change the human heart? Theft is a crime. It's a legal issue we can do something about, but start regulating how people feel? You've got a big problem there."

"I thought you said this place was on the verge of a riot. That's why we came here. Dexter could have handled graft and common theft," Robert accused.

Rupert defended his position. "There is talk of striking and burning down the general store. Racial hatred, murder, intimidating the miners—all this is being stirred up by someone. Mona, didn't you see some of that today when you talked with people?"

"I saw a lot I didn't like. I never expected a utopia in my mining village, but I expected a well-run operation where the miners and their families would have all their needs met plus a few luxuries here and there. This place is the opposite of what I wanted for the employees. The problem is how to proceed."

"I think we need a better plan than just sending Robert to the telegraph office. Sooner or later, you are going to be discovered, Mona. All we need is for your hat to blow off in the wind.

That platinum hair is a dead giveaway to your true identity," Rupert said.

Robert slopped stew on plates and put them on the table after filling the coffee cups. "This is the last of the coffee and rolls. Eat some stew and tell me what transpired today."

Mona hurriedly washed her hands from the water spilling out of the hand pump. It was frigid.

"Where are the baked goods promised?" Robert asked.

"We gave them to a couple who needed them more," Rupert said. "We'll get more bread in a couple of days."

Robert didn't reply, but sat down and silently ate his food.

Mona could tell he was upset. Robert understood they were in danger and was worried. Mona was glad he was with her as Robert was a good man to have one's back. She could trust her husband. Mona stabbed at her food. The stew was hot and filling as Mona sopped up the last of the gravy with the end of her roll.

As Rupert related to Robert the details of the day, Mona thought about an exit strategy. He was right. The three of them needed a better plan than just telegraphing Dexter.

Mona was not going to rest until they improvised a strategy to help her discover the secret behind the mayhem in Mooncrest Village. It looked like it was going to be a long night of planning. Mona was determined to shake the tree a little and see what fell out.

10

Mona tried not to yawn as she boarded the train to Alabama. She was worn out but at least was warmly dressed in her new clothes purchased in Mooncrest Village. She was still wearing her dark wig and sunglasses. Finding two empty seats in the coach section, she put her carryall case in the empty seat to save it.

Hearing the conductor yell, "ALL ABOARD! FINAL CALL!" Mona glanced anxiously out the window for Robert. She saw him come out of the station with Rupert following close behind. They spoke and then shook hands as the train began to move. She tapped apprehensively on the window, urging Robert to hurry.

Robert, seeing the train pulling away, ran and jumped onto the train steps, holding a battered suitcase that Rupert had given them to hold their city clothes. Like Mona, Robert wore the outfit she had purchased in Mooncrest Village and was grateful for its warmth. He found Mona in the coach car and put the makeup case in the rack above their heads as well as the battered suitcase.

Mona whispered, "I was worried you wouldn't make the train. What did Rupert say to you?"

"He said there was a man watching us and he followed you on the train. He's wearing a Stetson hat. See anyone familiar?"

"I'm afraid I don't know any employees from the mines except for the managers, but it is probably one of the men hired by my managers to keep tabs on suspicious characters coming into town."

"You put William Donovan to shame, Mona," Robert said, evoking President Roosevelt's gentleman spy.

"Lower your voice, Robert. Your English accent is a dead giveaway."

Robert chuckled. "I must learn to speak American. Hey wifey, let's go to the club car and see if he follows us."

Mona agreed. "I could do with a cup of tea."

Robert rose and allowed Mona to walk in front of him as they passed the stranger sporting a Stetson hat. They entered the club car and sat by a window. Mona asked for hot tea while Robert ordered a club soda. They munched on stale soda crackers left in a basket on the table.

"When will they start serving lunch?" Mona asked, thankful for the crackers.

"I'll ask the waiter, dear," Robert replied.

Several other people entered the car and took their seats. Mona and Robert exchanged glances.

"Maybe we were wrong about the man in the cowboy hat," Mona whispered.

The waiter served their drinks. "Sugar is on the table. Milk?"

Mona answered, "No, thank you. This will do. Um, when will the dining car open?"

The waiter answered, "The dining car will be open at 11:30, ma'am."

"Thank you." Mona glanced up as the car door opened again.

The suspected Moon Mine detective walked in, searched the car and upon seeing Mona and Robert, took a seat where he could observe them. The man, sporting a dark suit with a bolo tie with a large, turquoise stone and brown boots, still wore his Stetson hat. If the man was a detective, he made no effort to blend in with the other passengers.

"Robert, don't turn around, but he's here," Mona said, stirring her tea and glancing at the man occasionally.

"How do you want to play this?" Robert asked, facing away from the man.

"Leave him be. Let's give him nothing to report. We're just a boring couple visiting their cousin and now returning home."

"If you want me to thump him, just give the word."

Mona sat back in her chair and giggled.

"What are you laughing at?"

"You. Oh, I wish I had a camera. You should see yourself. You look like Paul Bunyon with your red plaid shirt, work pants, fur-lined trapper hat with flaps covering your ears. Can you take the hat off, please?"

Robert pulled off his rabbit-lined hat. "Forgot I had it on. Keeps my ears warm."

"Wet down your hair, Robert. It's sticking straight up."

Robert licked his fingers and tried to smooth down his hair.

Mona leaned over the table to help.

Robert asked, "What's he doing now?"

"Pretending he is reading a newspaper, but the man is watching us for sure. There may be others on the train following us, but he was the one we spotted. He's so bad at this."

"Only ten other people got on the train the same time we did."

"Agents could have gotten on the train further up the line."

Robert suggested, "Let's be careful. I'll go through all the compartments and try to remember faces. We'll see if anyone who boarded with us is on the train after we reach Wyoming."

"We have stopped at every small town on the line. It's frustrating. How long is it going to take to get to Sheridan?"

Robert answered, "I don't know, dear. Might be tomorrow until we reach Sheridan. This means we have to sleep in coach. I would love to have a stateroom with a private bath."

Mona took a deep breath, kidding, "Me, too, but we can't afford a stateroom on your farm equipment salesman salary, dear."

"All right, Mrs. Maplewood. Eat your crackers and drink your tea. It's several hours before the dining car opens."

When Mona and Robert finished their drinks, they left the club car, but not before Mona passed the detective and dropped her purse in front of him.

Startled, the detective retrieved the purse and handed it back to her. "Here you go, ma'am."

Mona noticed the man had a milky eye. "Thank you. I'm all sixes and sevens today."

The man nodded and went back to reading his paper.

Mona and Robert left the club car and went back to the coach car only to find their seats had been usurped. Resigned to sit apart, Mona took a seat next to an elderly woman who had been visiting her daughter in Helena, Montana and was going home to South Dakota.

Robert took the opportunity to walk through all the passenger cars and finally went back to the club car to smoke.

The man with the Stetson hat was gone.

Robert ordered tomato juice and took his time

smoking several cigarettes. Feeling refreshed, he went in search of the "Stetson" man. He found the man sitting several rows behind Mona on the opposite side of the aisle, listening to her spin a tale of visiting her cousin in Montana who worked for the Moon Enterprises Mining Corporation to the elderly woman. Robert took a seat several rows behind the man in western getup and was relieved when the man got off at Billings, Montana.

Mona's elderly companion went to the dining car, so Robert sat next to Mona again. Mona looked relieved as she asked, "Where have you been?"

"Watching our friend watching you, but he's left the train."

Mona replied, "That doesn't mean someone else is not watching us."

He replied, "True, but you'll be happy to know that I talked to the conductor and got us a stateroom with a couple of berths. Won't be ready until the afternoon though. They have to clean it."

Mona grabbed his arm. "Oh, did you really? Now we don't have to sit up all night?"

Robert wrapped her arm around his as Mona rested her head on his shoulder. "Great way to spend a honeymoon. I'm exhausted, dirty, and hungry."

"I'll make it up to you, Mr. Maplewood."

"You better."

"I'm just gonna close my eyes for a minute. You take point." Mona did close her eyes and quickly fell asleep as did Robert. When they awoke, they discovered that they had slept through lunch and the dining car was now closed until dinner. With stomachs growling, they trod back to the club car where they munched on peanuts, popcorn, and pretzels left on the bar counter while sipping on tomato juice.

The past week was enough to give a person an ulcer, and Mona was sure she was getting one.

11

It was early the next morning when the train crawled into Sheridan, Wyoming. Very few people got off the train besides Mona and Robert. The two hung about the depot as if waiting for their family to see if anyone was watching. After concluding they were not being followed, Mona and Robert hailed a cab and asked to be taken to a nice hotel.

The cab driver pulled up in front of a three-story, red brick hotel which had a café on the first floor. Robert paid the driver and helped Mona out of the cab. She was a little stiff after sitting on the train for a day. The hotel's foyer was nothing special, but it was clean. Mona went to the desk clerk's counter and requested a room with a shower.

The clerk replied that only the bridal suite included a bathroom—all the other rooms shared a bathroom on the floor.

"We'll take it," Mona said, registering as Mr. and Mrs. Maplewood.

"It's awfully expensive. It's five dollars a night," the desk clerk said, looking to see if Mona wore a wedding ring. He thought that Mona and Robert looked like they had been riding the rails as hobos with their lumberjack attire and muddy boots.

Robert pulled out his wallet and gave a twenty-dollar bill to the clerk. "This should cover several days. Now, my good man, do you have room service?"

Flummoxed that Robert had casually produced twenty dollars from his wallet during a depression, the clerk held the bill up to the light. Deciding the money looked legit, the clerk gulped before speaking, "Everyone comes down to the café."

Robert pulled out a tenner and stuffed it in the clerk's vest pocket. "Well, starting today, the bridal suite includes room service. We want two steaks, cooked medium, two baked potatoes with lots of butter, two house salads, two orange juices, a pot of hot tea, and a pot of coffee. I'll expect it in twenty minutes."

Stunned, the clerk tugged at his collar, muttering as he handed over the room keys, "Yes, sir."

Mona took one of the keys, asking the clerk. "Is there a drugstore nearby?"

"Around the corner, ma'am."

Mona said to Robert, "See you in a bit. I'm going to get us a few things."

"Don't be long."

"I won't, dearest. I'll be as quick as I can."

Mona followed the clerk's directions and found the drugstore easily. Fortunately, the drugstore had what she was really seeking—a telephone booth. Not wanting to make the call from the hotel where nosy switchboard operators could listen in, Mona needed another avenue to a telephone. Quickly closing the phone booth door, Mona made a collect call to Dexter Deatherage, her attorney.

His secretary accepted the long-distance charges, warmly greeted Mona, and asked her to hold for Mr. Deatherage. In less than a minute, Dexter was on the line listening to Mona giving him a coded message. He responded by asking for the safe word. This was a word Mona would give to verify her identity as Mona Moon and to assure him that she was safe. If she had been in danger, she would have used another word.

Responding to the code word, Dexter replied, "Give me four days."

"Make it three. We are sitting on a potential powder keg."

"We'll see what we can do," Dexter said before hanging up.

Satisfied, Mona hung the phone back on the receiver and left the booth. Hoping the café was close to delivering her meal, Mona hurriedly purchased a few odds and ends before leaving. She wanted nothing more than an edible meal, a hot shower, and lots of sleep.

Mona was so exhausted she believed she could sleep for days.

And she did.

12

Four days later in Sheridan, Robert and Mona left their hotel for the train station. They climbed aboard private rail cars heading for Butte, Montana. Dexter Deatherage stood as they entered the car. Violet, Mona's maid and companion, was present as well, rounding out the Moon Manor entourage. There was a little extra bonus for Mona as Violet had brought Chloe, Mona's white Standard Poodle. Upon seeing her, Chloe barked excitedly and jumped into Mona's arms.

Mona hugged the squirming dog and pressed her face into Chloe's fur. "Oh, you smell so good," Mona blurted.

"I gave her a bath before we left," Violet said, smiling.

Mona set Chloe down and pressed Violet's hand. "It was so good of you to come on such short notice. Dexter explained that this might be a dangerous mission?"

Violet said, "I want to help, Miss Mona."

"As long as you know what you're getting into," Robert said.

Dexter said, "Violet and the Pinkerton men know as much as I do. I didn't hold anything back. They know the importance of the copper mines. The mines are the financial backbone of Moon Enterprises. If the problems at the mines can be fixed, we want to assist in any way possible."

Mona felt her heart beat with pride. "Bless you all for coming as I don't know what awaits us. I'll tell you what I saw during my stay with Rupert Hunt. Let's sit down. This may take a while."

Dexter and Violet obliged and listened without interrupting as Mona related what she had witnessed in the Mooncrest Village. When she had finished, the two glanced at each other. They understood the strategy of stirring up racial tensions. They hoped their status as Mona's personal employees would protect them from harm as they knew they would not be welcomed by many factions in Butte or Mooncrest Village.

"I can do some undercover sleuthing for you, Miss Mona."

"How so, Violet?"

"Once Mr. Deatherage told me what was happening, I brought all sorts of patterns with me. We can have an old-fashioned sewing cotillion with me handing out patterns and yakking it up with the ladies. I believe a few would confide in me."

Mona shook her head. "Violet, I won't hear of you giving away your patterns which you have spent years collecting."

Violet was adamant. "The ladies can copy my patterns. Why can't we stop for a few hours in Butte before we head to Mooncrest Village? I'm sure they have a Five and Dime store where I can purchase patterns and bolts of cloth as well."

Dexter said, "That might not be a bad idea, Mona. Violet can insinuate herself with ladies."

Mona didn't agree at first. "They are good suggestions, but I was thinking more of having a tea for the women. Let me think about it, Dexter.

What did you tell the mine managers?"

"I sent a telegram that you had changed your honeymoon plans and would be visiting the mines ostensibly to show your new husband."

"Do you think they suspect they are being investigated, Dexter?"

"I think they were surprised that you are coming, but not suspicious. They'll be waiting when you arrive at the Butte train station."

"What about the Pinkertons?"

Dexter replied, "They've been quietly arriving in groups of no more than two for days now since you telegrammed. Some have applied to the mines for various positions. Others are staying in different hotels with various cover stories they are telling the hotel's management. I have held back a bodyguard detail of six who will stick with you."

"Dexter, won't the mine's management be suspicious about a security detail?"

Scratching his chin, Dexter said, "Ever since the Alice Stoll kidnapping, everyone knows the rich take extra precautions now. I don't think they'll wonder anything about it."

Mona agreed as the recent kidnapping of tycoon Alice Speed Stoll from her own home in Louisville had been a shocking affair. "Okay, we've got a day before we arrive in Butte. Let's work on getting our strategy straight."

Mona, Robert, Violet, and Dexter put their heads together, thinking of how to attack the problems at Moon Mine. However, Mona considered the murder of the miner Piotr Wojcik to be an isolated incident and not a symptom of the mine's problems.

Only time would tell if Mona was correct.

13

Mona stepped off the train first with Robert following. She was wearing a double-breasted navy overcoat with oversized copper buttons and a copper belt. The coat spilled over her navy trousers and black boots while its high collar was perched upward, accenting her swan-like neck. Mona also wore long navy gloves with copper buttons going up one side. She adjusted her jaunty Fedora sporting a veil with one hand while clutching her Schiaparelli navy handbag which boasted a copper clasp.

Mona looked rich, commanding, and formidable as the three mine managers presented her with several bouquets of flowers. She handed the flowers to Violet before shaking their hands as they doffed their hats in the blustery wind. "You remember my husband, Robert Farley, Duke of Brynelleth."

They gave little nods with their chins and shook Robert's hands.

Next Mona introduced Dexter to the group. "And you remember my lawyer, Dexter Deatherage."

The managers appeared a little stunned at the appearance of Mona's personal attorney, but quickly recovered, heartily greeting Dexter. It was obvious Dexter had not informed them that he would be accompanying Mona when he notified them of her visit.

Holding onto his hat, Robert said, "Can we get out of this wind, gentlemen?"

"Of course. Of course," all three muttered. They directed Mona and Robert to a black Packard with the Moon Enterprises logo on the side. They made to enter the car as well, but Mona asked them to take one of the Ford sedans parked behind the Packard. Instead, she motioned for Violet and Chloe to take a seat in the car. "Dexter, you ride with these nice gentlemen and have them bring you up to date on the mines."

Dexter tried not to smile. Mona had struck the first blow by letting the managers know that she, in no uncertain terms, called the shots—not them. It was obvious the three managers were taken aback at Mona's display of authority. Dexter patted one of the managers on the back and said to them, "Join me in my car. You can let me off at the hotel on your way back to your offices."

One of the managers said, "But I thought we were going to spend time with Mrs. Farley to discuss the mines."

Dexter answered, "Yes, I want to remind you in matters concerning anything to do with Moon Enterprises, Mona Moon Farley will still be addressed as Miss Moon."

"What?" the managers echoed, confused.

Mona's lawyer explained, "It has to do with her uncle's wishes and the terms of the will. Just think of it as a stage name or how those movie stars do it in Hollywood. As for discussions concerning the mines, Miss Moon intends on doing that, but she'll want to rest first. Miss Moon will contact you when she is ready to meet with you."

The three managers glanced at each other but having no other recourse, jumped into the Ford with Dexter.

The Farleys and Violet arrived at the Hotel Finlen, a French empire style, red-brick, nine-story building where Dexter had reserved an entire floor for Mona and her staff. It was easier to maintain security if the Pinkertons didn't have to keep an eye on other guests taking rooms on the floor. They locked the empty rooms and did not allow hotel staff unless they were accompanied by a Pinkerton.

Robert escorted his wife into the hotel and up to the registration desk as six of the Pinkertons piled into the lobby. Violet stood behind the couple trying to control Chloe, who wanted to sniff everything, straining against her leash.

In his very posh, upper-class English accent, Robert greeted the hotel clerk. "Hello, my good man. I am the Duke of Brynelleth. This is my wife, the Duchess of Brynelleth. She is to be addressed as Your Grace in the English style or Miss Mona in the Southern style. I'm afraid we've had to make some accommodations regarding my wife's salutations. I hope you understand. She's an American, you know."

The clerk looked back and forth between Robert and Mona. "We'll do our best sir, I mean, Your Grace."

"Very good. I believe you have our rooms ready."

Upon hearing Robert's upper class English accent, the entire front desk staff plus the switchboard operators emerged from their office located behind the front counter and stood around the clerk waiting on the Farleys, wanting to see the famous society couple. "Please sign here," the clerk replied, his voice shaking just a bit. "All is in readiness, Your Grace."

Robert signed their names in the registration book and said, "How tickety-boo. The rest of our staff will arrive shortly."

"Very good, Your Grace." The clerk handed keys to ten rooms over to Robert who handed them to a Pinkerton. Immediately, three Pinkertons went to the elevators. They were to search each room before giving Robert *the okay.*

Robert glanced at his watch and turned back to the clerk. "Where might we obtain elevenses?"

The clerk glanced at his co-workers for a

translation. "What's that, Your Grace?"

Mona deadpanned, "His Grace is inquiring about food. He's hungry. He's English, you know. The English have to eat every two hours or they perish from the lack of nourishment. They have breakfast, then elevenses. Once they are finished with elevenses, they have lunch, then tea, and then supper, which may last until ten at night because of the many courses served. Besides eating, the English upper-class gentlemen spend their time hunting and chasing house maids." She turned to Robert. "No offense, dear."

"None taken, darling," Robert answered.

The clerk weakly said, "The dining room is open."

Needing a cup of tea badly and perhaps a buttered roll, Robert said, "Very good. Come, dear. Come Violet."

The clerk opened his mouth to announce the hotel's policy of no dogs in the dining area but thought better of it.

"Thank you," Mona told the clerk, amused at Robert and the clerk's exchange. She turned and strolled with Robert to the dining hall as the clerk, scratching his head, watched them retreat. She and Robert smiled at each other, knowing vivid accounts of their arrival would be all over the city of Butte before the half-hour was up. They had wanted to put the first step of their plan into place by creating a stir.

Hearing the hubbub, the hotel manager came out from his private office to see his entire front desk staff gawking at Robert and Mona. He clapped his hands and everyone scurried. Of course, he too stood, watching the Farleys saunter into the dining room. He hoped they wouldn't be a problem, but deep in his heart, he knew they would be.

They just looked like trouble.

14

"Thank you for having us," Mona said, wearing a long-sleeved, black velvet dress with a high neckline accentuated by a long strand of pearls underneath a velvet cape. She looked stunning.

"It's our pleasure," Mrs. Montrose replied. "George, help Miss Mona off with her coat . . . I mean her cape."

"Allow me, Mr. Montrose." Robert interjected as he gently slid the cape off Mona's shoulders taking care not to disturb his wife's coifed tresses.

Mr. Montrose, general manager of Moon Enterprises Mining Corp, accepted the cape and handed it to a maid.

Mrs. Montrose escorted Mona to the drawing room. "I hope you don't mind, but I've invited a few locals to dine with us. You know, I'm surprised you decided to come to Montana. When we attended your wedding, I thought you were sailing to Europe for your honeymoon."

Mona gave a quick smile, saying, "We have postponed the trip for now."

Obviously disappointed that Mona would not elaborate, Mrs. Montrose ushered the famous couple into a vast drawing room where a baker's dozen of Butte's finest citizens sat in eager anticipation of the famous couple's arrival. "May I present the Duke and Duchess of Brynelleth, Mona and Robert Farley."

Everyone stood.

"Please call me Mona."

Robert deadpanned, "You may refer to me as *Your Grace*. I'm not as liberal as my American wife."

The guests twittered as it was well known Robert Farley was a stuffed shirt.

"You remember Greg Bannock, manager of Mooncrest Village?" Mrs. Montrose said. "Mamie is his charming wife."

Mona replied, "Of course, I remember. We met at my wedding and then again this morning."

"How do you do?" Mamie Bannock asked.

"Very well. Thank you for asking." Mona noticed that Mamie, sporting a faint mustache and overly-plucked eyebrows, shuddered a bit when Mona threw out her hand to shake.

Seeing his wife's response, Mr. Bannock grabbed Mona's fingers and gave them a kiss, just barely touching in the European fashion of greeting. He said, "You are enchanting as always, Miss Mona. Mamie and I so enjoyed your wedding celebration and are glad we can entertain you now. How was the train ride?"

"Exhausting, but I got a good nap in this afternoon." Mona gave a quick glance at Mamie who was chugging down a glass of champagne before moving on.

Mrs. Montrose introduced another couple, "This is Mr. and Mrs. Charles Lacoste. Mr. Lacoste is the general manager for the offices of Moon Enterprises Mining Corp."

George Montrose quickly added, "Yes, Charles oversees the executive offices for the mines while I run the mines themselves."

Mona nodded, "I make it a point to remember all my managers and their functions, but thank you for reminding me. Nice to meet you all again, George."

Mrs. Montrose gave her husband a sharp look. "No shoptalk tonight. I forbid it."

"I'm with you there, Mrs. Montrose," Robert quipped. "Please introduce me to the rest of your illustrious guests." He extended his arm to Mrs. Montrose and escorted her to the middle of the room, where she introduced Robert to the mayor of Butte, a governor's aid, several ministers, and their wives. Mr. Montrose gave his arm to Mona, which she accepted. She purposely walked slowly.

This gave Mona a few seconds to study the room and count the servants. She paid her managers a princely sum to live very comfortably, but not to inhabit a mansion almost as grand as Moon Manor and have five servants standing in attendance. She wondered how many servants were in the kitchen and upstairs.

The furniture in Mrs. Montrose's home looked new and expensive, showing no signs of wear and the walls smelled of fresh paint. Mona studied Mrs. Montrose's blue-black beaded dress. While not European haute couture, the dress was expensive and made by an experienced dressmaker. It must have cost a pretty penny as the beads had to be sewn on by hand.

As she shook the guests' hands, Mona took note of everyone's watches and jewelry. The Moon managers and their wives were wearing expensive watches and baubles, none of which were paste. Mona made a mental list of the necklaces, earrings, and bracelets. She would have Rupert Hunt investigate the purchase of such items. It could be that the jewels were on loan. Mona hoped for the managers' sakes that they were.

15

Rupert was waiting for Mona and Robert in their suite. He and Violet were playing catch with Chloe when the couple strode in. Upon seeing Mona, Chloe dropped her ball and rushed over to Mona.

"Watch the pearls! Watch the pearls!" Mona admonished, not wanting Chloe's paws to become entangled with the loop. She pulled the long strand of pearls over her head and handed them to Violet before patting Chloe and throwing her ball.

"Well, how was it?" Rupert asked.

Robert spoke up, "Before you two get into it, I'm going to bed. Mona, don't be too long."

Mona replied, "I won't, dear. Just need to go over a few things with Rupert."

"Shall I stay up, Miss Mona?" Violet asked.

"If you want to, but feel free to retire. I don't want to keep you up as it is late."

"No problem," Violet said happily, looking back and forth between Rupert and Mona. She liked to be in on things.

Rupert admonished, "Everything said here is confidential, baby doll."

Violet shot him a haughty look. "I realize that, Rupert."

"Rupert?"

The spy swung his head around to Mona. "Yes?"

"I asked you and Dexter to do a background check on my mine managers. What are Montrose, Bannock, and Lacoste receiving as compensation?"

"The same as the last time you checked the payroll books, Mona. They each receive two thousand five hundred dollars to run the Moon copper mines with perks like company cars, vacation pay, and other benefits. Montrose handles the mines, Lacoste handles the offices, and Bannock does the accounts plus payroll. Dexter and I checked into their backgrounds and found some interesting items."

"Such as?"

"It's Montrose who seems to be the most interesting of the three. He lives well above his means. He drives a flashy Cord Phaeton, gives freely to charitable causes, and is in debt to the bank for five thousand dollars. It seems Mrs. Montrose is behind this extravagance as she wants to become one of the swells. She is known as a social climber."

Mona asked, "The other two?"

"Live more modestly. Bannock and Lacoste drink only at social occasions, no girlfriends, but play handsies with their secretaries when they think they can get away with it, go to church on Sundays, eat meatloaf on Mondays, play croquet with the kiddies, go to baseball games in the summertime, and the movies once a week—never miss a day of work. In other words, typical middle-aged, white-collar men."

"Is that all?"

Rupert replied, "I did find out Bannock likes to play poker with the boys twice a month."

"Who are the *boys*?"

"Fellows you don't want to meet in a dark

alley. The lower echelon of Butte society, you might say. Bannock likes to slum."

Mona absent-mindedly scratched her cheek. "Let's talk about the miners."

Rupert pulled a notebook from his breast pocket. "Nationally, the average wage for un-skilled labor is 45 cents per hour. Moon Enterprises raises that to 60 cents if a person has been employed for six months. The average wage for a miner is $4.49 per day for 10 hour days, six days a week. Moon Enterprises pays $5.50 per day for an 8 hour shift, five days a week, so the pay between Moon mines and other mines works out to the non-Moon miners making more money, but the men work themselves to death. The pay for skilled Moon miners is significantly higher than other mines and men can make about $1700 per annum, which is considered very good pay. In addition, Moon Enterprises Mining Corporation, which is a subsidiary of Moon Enterprises, is supposed to offer its miners food at cost, free medical care, free housing, and other benefits. Other mining corporations offer fewer benefits, but they deliver regarding their contracts with employees. Moon Enterprises is not delivering on its promises."

Mona asked, "How many men are on my payroll?"

"One hundred and two men plus four women. They all work in various capacities. Two hundred and thirty-one souls live in Mooncrest Village alone. Believe me when I say these people are not the problem at the mines. It is rooted in mismanagement or outside agitation. I haven't discovered the cause yet."

"Could the Wobblies be stirring up things?"

"I think the IWW movement is still active in this area. However, most workers got tired of the violence. Too many deaths. If the miners strike, it will be without major assistance from the IWW."

"Have you seen any IWW pamphlets or symbols about?" Mona wondered out loud.

"The black cat symbol of the IWW for sabotage hasn't been discovered around here for years. That's why I think the IWW isn't involved at the Moon mines, even though I think some of the Wobblies and a handful of old timers are still around."

Mona listened carefully to her spy. "Okay—I'll put the IWW aside for the moment. Let's get back to the managers. I want to know how Montrose could acquire such expensive accouterments on his salary. Montrose should be able to live in a very nice house, send his children to private school, afford a cook and a maid, and buy some custom dresses for his wife—not purchase haute couture and employ the number of servants we encountered. What I saw was a five thousand a year income."

Rupert agreed. "Twenty-five hundred a year is a very nice living nowadays, but not the way Montrose lives."

Mona handed him a list. "These are the jewels the wives were wearing. Only the managers' wives—not the other guests present."

"They could have rented those jewels to impress you, Miss Mona," Violet offered.

"I've thought of that, but I certainly don't recall seeing them wear such finery at my wedding, which is where they would have put on the dog. I can see the ladies borrowing jewels as to pay respect, so I need to know the truth before I make any accusations. It was that the jewels were of a modern design—not inherited pieces."

Violet sounded concerned, "They could have

had older pieces remounted."

Mona nodded. "I know, Violet. That is why I want it investigated. Believe me when I say we won't make any accusations without concrete proof. I know it sounds snobbish of me to complain about these jewels when I have so many pretty trinkets, but if you could have witnessed the deprivation of the miners, you would be wondering where all the profits from the mines are going, too."

Glancing at the list, Rupert said, "I'll have men check the Butte and Helena jewelry stores for information. I also have a handsome young chap chatting up a maid at the Montrose house. If there is something hinky going on there, we'll find out."

"Do you have the report on the death of the miner Piotr Wojcik?"

Rupert handed Mona a file, which Mona quickly perused.

"I'm not going to ask how you got this report," Mona said while studying the few pages along with newspaper clippings.

"It's better if you don't."

Mona concluded, "There's no autopsy report here."

"The police didn't order one. They noted that he was stabbed and listed it as the manner of Wojcik's demise on his death certificate."

Mona kept reading. "It says here that Wojcik was killed in Butte. I thought he was murdered in Mooncrest Village."

"The fight between Wojcik and this Indian took place in Mooncrest Village, but Wojcik was killed in Butte."

"Did either man have access to a vehicle?"

"Not that I'm aware of."

"No mention of transportation for either man." Mona closed the folder. "So, tell me, Rupert, how two men could have traversed a slushy, icy road in the dark from Mooncrest Village thirty miles to Butte without help? There is not even any speculation about how they both got into Butte in this report?"

Rupert grinned. "You're now beginning to see the cogs within cogs."

"Isn't that wheels within wheels?" Violet asked.

"Don't confuse the issues, honey babe," Rupert spat out at Violet. "You both know what I'm saying."

"Stop it, you two. We've got some grave issues here."

Violet said, "Sorry, Miss Mona. I know this is serious."

"Rupert, have you found any connection of Piotr Wojcik to a competitor's mine? Had he worked for anyone else before coming to us?"

"He once worked for the Anaconda Mine."

Mona was irritated. "I gave strict instructions that we were not to hire from competing mines, especially the Anaconda Mine."

Rupert shrugged, pushing Chloe's wet nose away. "Again, that's a question for Montrose. I don't do the hiring and firing."

Mona asked, "What kind of man was Wojcik?"

"A hard-working man. A drinker. He liked to pick on smaller fellows."

"In other words—a bully."

Rupert answered, "Some would say so."

Mona flipped over a letter from the folder and read it. "I see that he had taken out insurance with us. Have we paid the death benefit?"

"I don't know. Take it up with Lacoste or Deatherage."

"What about this Indian? What was his name?"

"A typical Blackfoot by the name of Jeb Wheedle."

"Wheedle? Like Bill Wheedle we gave the baked goods to?"

"They are cousins."

Mona asked, "What kind of Indian name is Wheedle?"

"It isn't. They don't like to give us their Indian names. Rather private thing for them, so they give us names given to them by Christian missionaries."

"You said Mr. Wheedle was a typical Blackfoot. What does that mean?"

"*Reserved* would be a word I would use. They keep to themselves. They have to tread two worlds—the Indian and the white world. Life is not easy for them. I have Wheedle's work report in the file. No major infractions or insubordination."

"You said that Wojcik grabbed Mr. Wheedle's medicine bundle."

"That's what started the fight. Wojcik was always riding Wheedle."

Mona asked, "How did Mr. Wheedle react to Mr. Wojcik's bullying?"

"Usually, Wheedle walked away or he just took it, but the grabbing of his medicine pouch was too much. Wheedle exploded."

"Who won the fight?"

"Wheedle gave as good as he got, but the two men were pulled apart before the finish. I think Wheedle would have beaten Wojcik to the ground if the other men hadn't interfered."

"Were both men drunk?"

Rupert answered, "Yep."

"Alcohol is not allowed in Mooncrest Village. Where did they get the juice?"

"Otto sells bootlegged whiskey out of the back of the store."

Mona closed her eyes, murmuring, "That's just lovely."

Rupert threw a ball for Chloe before asking Mona, "We still on for tomorrow?"

"Yes, Montrose and Bannock will pick us up at 10:30 for an inspection at Mooncrest Village. Are the supply trucks all set?"

Rupert answered, "Dexter and I will pick up the supplies at ten o'clock. You know I feel like you are putting a carrot before the miners, prodding them like mules."

"I am extending an olive branch and establishing trust."

"If you say so, but don't expect them to be grateful."

Undeterred, Mona asked, "What about the Pinkertons?"

Rupert said, "They'll be ready if there is a problem with the miners. They've been warned to dress like the miners and not to bring weapons like slapjacks and brass knuckles. Be prepared if you're not exactly welcome, Mona. I think Mr. Montrose has something unpleasant up his sleeve."

Mona explained, "I realize there is going to be some resentment. I hope to put a damper on that with my visit."

"We shall see tomorrow then."

Mona grinned. "I had a lot of pushback from the managers. For some reason it seemed they didn't want me to visit Mooncrest Village."

Rupert returned a grin. "I wonder why."

Mona advised, "Tomorrow is going to be a hard day for everyone."

Rupert rose. "I'm going down the hall to sleep. Like you said, Mona—it's going to be a rough day tomorrow regardless of the outcome." He quietly closed the door when leaving.

Violet said, "I'm ready as well."

"There's bound to be violence tomorrow, Violet. I would prefer if you stayed at the hotel with Chloe."

"I think our plan will be a success tomorrow. I'm not afraid. I want to help."

"Let's hope so, Violet. I need to break through the miners' wall of silence."

Violet yawned and then clapped her mouth, giggling. "So sorry."

Mona rose. "I know you're tired. Go to bed."

Violet rose also and pressed Mona's hand. "Tomorrow will be a success. You'll see. You've never lost a battle yet." Violet gave Mona one last smile before heading to her own room.

Following Violet, Mona peered out into the hallway, checking that a Pinkerton was guarding the elevator. She locked the suite door and checked the windows before she sat at a desk and made out a list of everything she wanted to accomplish. Glancing at the clock, she saw it was two in the morning. Yawning, she went into the bedroom where she found Robert asleep, slightly snoring. Throwing her evening gown on a chair, she and Chloe jumped into bed, and all three were soon at rest in the arms of Morpheus.

16

The next morning, Montrose and Lacoste joined Mona's group aboard a rented Packard Touring car, which was used for excursions in national parks. Bannock was the last to arrive and seated himself in the last row in the touring car, which boasted five seat benches and could hold twenty passengers.

Seeing an opportunity in the conversation, Mona turned around in her seat and asked, "Who is responsible for Mooncrest Village and the roads?"

Montrose pointed to Lacoste sitting next to him.

"That would be me, Miss Moon," Lacoste answered.

Mona remarked, "I see fresh gravel has been

poured on the road."

"We have to replace the gravel ever so often. The ore trucks are so heavy, they grind the gravel into the dirt."

Mona asked, "How often is the road serviced?"

"Snow and slush is the biggest problem we have. The roads are cleared as needed."

Irritated by Lacoste's vague, evasive answers, Mona demanded, "Can you be a little more specific about what 'as needed' means?"

"Well, we remove the snow after it falls as soon as possible."

"Does that mean within eight hours, 24 hours, two days, two weeks? What does 'as soon as possible' mean, Mr. Lacoste? It's a simple question."

Montrose leaned forward. "We make sure the ore goes to the smelters on schedule."

Frustrated at the managers' lack of transparency, Mona turned around in her seat, fuming and remained silent until Bannock asked, "Miss Moon, why are three trucks following us?"

"Yes, what is their purpose?" Montrose echoed.

"You'll see," was Mona's equally vague response. She could be cryptic as well. Turning to Violet sitting next to her, Mona squeezed her hand. When would this ride ever end?

After a bumpy forty-five minute ride, Mona finally saw Mooncrest Village. "Stop the bus," she ordered the driver.

He stopped at the entrance to the little mining town. Violet got out and jumped into the cab of one of the trucks, which then sped directly onto the road leading to the miners' housing.

Montrose asked, "What's going on, Miss Moon? I demand an answer."

"You what?" Mona angrily turned around in her seat. "You demand nothing. You watch your viper's tongue, sir."

Bannock, wishing to defuse the tension, said, "Miss Moon, we have built a platform for your speech. We've even set up a microphone. You can see the miners are waiting for you."

"I am not going to address the miners. At least, not today."

"Then why are we here, Miss Moon?" Lacoste asked.

"To establish goodwill and to inspect the village, but I have no intention of standing before a group of hostile men and risk being hit by rotten eggs and rough words."

Bannock exclaimed, "We never would dream of allowing such a thing!"

Mona retorted sarcastically, "Of course not, gentlemen. Such a thing never would have crossed your mind. Mr. Lacoste, you will announce on your fine microphone that they are to return to their houses where they will receive free supplies—courtesy of Mona Moon, owner of Moon Enterprises Mining Corp. Then you will invite all the women from age sixteen and up to have tea with me at two o'clock at the community center. No men allowed."

Aghast that his carefully laid plans for Mona's visit had disintegrated, Lacoste had no choice but to acquiesce. The man was afraid of being fired if he objected. It seemed Mona Moon was on the warpath, and he was not going to take any chances of losing his job during a depression.

Hearing a muffled guffaw, Lacoste noticed Robert Farley's shoulders shook as though the man was silently laughing at him. Lacoste felt like a fool and shot a hateful look at the other two managers sitting with him. They had concocted a plan to control Mona's visit but it seemed they had been bested. Lacoste worried about what the day would bring. Having no choice, Lacoste answered, "Yes, Miss Moon. Whatever you say."

"That's right, gentlemen." Mona crooked her arm around Robert's, saying, "Whatever I say. Driver, go on to the store and park in the back, please."

The driver released the brake and put the touring car in first gear and then second, going slowly up the remaining hill to the mining store.

There was total silence as the passengers disembarked the car and entered the store, except for Mr. Lacoste who walked down the slope to announce to the miners to go back home and invite the women to tea.

It was clear Mona would win the propaganda battle this day.

17

Mona entered the store by the back door, followed by Robert, then the managers and lastly, Mona's handpicked security team. She checked out the storage room before visiting Otto's office. Everything looked neat and tidy.

"May I assist you?" Mr. Bannock asked, nervously, poking his head inside Otto's office.

Mona turned around. "You're sweating, Mr. Bannock."

Mr. Bannock reached for his handkerchief and patted his forehead. "Am I? It's so warm today."

Robert mentioned, "No, it's not, old man. It's below thirty outside."

"I mean the store is warm."

"It's not that either," Robert replied, wandering off.

Wiping the back of his neck, Bannock followed Robert out to the store's display floor. Mona, Mr. Montrose, and the security team followed suit.

Several muscular men stood behind the counter corralling Otto, who looked beseechingly at Bannock and Montrose.

"What's going on here?" Montrose said, outraged. "Who are those men with Otto?"

Mona replied, "They are my employees, Mr. Montrose, just like you. Please don't interfere."

"But . . . ?" Montrose protested.

Mona held up her hand. "I said not to interfere. I'm not going to warn you again." She whispered something to one of the Pinkertons encircling Otto.

The man nodded and he and his partner dragged Otto out the back way into a waiting car.

"Where are you taking Otto?" Mr. Montrose demanded.

Mona replied, "None of your concern." She strode about the store picking up an article or two and inspecting them. "Gentlemen, this store will be closed until further notice. There is a car waiting to take you fine fellows back to Butte."

"What car? I didn't hear a car," Bannock said, looking out the front window.

"Nevertheless, there is a car waiting for you in the back of the store. Take my advice and leave at once."

"But you need us to assist you, Miss Moon. The miners are hostile," Mr. Montrose said, frantically.

Mona replied, "If they were so hostile, why did you plan on me speaking before them? That would have put me in danger. I never authorized making a speech before the miners."

Bannock offered, "We thought it would give you a chance to explain your side of things to them."

Mona laughed bitterly. "You mean getting screamed at, called nasty names, and perhaps shot. Which one of you hired someone to agitate them into an angry mob? I saw some of the men carrying clubs and bats."

Mr. Montrose said, "I didn't see anything untoward. No one was carrying weapons."

"Are you saying I imagined this?"

Montrose locked eyes with Mona and then lowered his to avoid her fierce glare. "I must be mistaken."

"I will not talk to the miners now, but I think they will calm down once their womenfolk are on board with me. I've invited them to the community center."

"How do you mean?" Mr. Bannock asked.

"At this very moment a high tea is being set up for the women of the Mooncrest Village. I will speak to the women."

Mr. Bannock said, "They won't come."

"I think most will, Mr. Bannock—out of curiosity if nothing else."

"They won't come because they have nothing decent to wear," Mr. Bannock retorted.

Mona turned to him. "You mean I pay the highest wages in the business, and the wives don't have one decent frock to wear to a tea. That doesn't sound right to me."

Bannock wiped his mouth with his handkerchief, knowing that he had said the wrong thing.

"That's not all I've done, gentleman. Right now, Violet and Mr. Deatherage are distributing ten pounds of flour, ten pounds of sugar, 2 pounds of coffee, 24 fresh eggs, five pounds of butter, 2 gallons of buttermilk, 1 gallon of cooking oil, ten pounds of potatoes, five pounds of onions, one can of baking soda, one can of salt, one can of baking powder, one can of peanut butter, and one bottle of vanilla and orange extract at each doorstep. Each child will receive a bag with five peppermint sticks, five licorice whips, five assorted suckers along with a skipping rope and a yo-yo."

"That's what the trucks were for?" accused Mr. Bannock. "You're bribing them."

"I am righting a wrong, Mr. Bannock. You three are to go to your homes and wait for my call. You are not to go to your offices until further notice nor speak with each other. Be forewarned that my men will be monitoring your homes."

Mr. Bannock cried out, "What have we done to deserve so dastardly a treatment from you? We've worked our fingers to the bone for you."

"This is outrageous!" Mr. Montrose complained. "I will not be treated this way."

"Then resign, Mr. Montrose," Mona replied.

Mr. Montrose made a sudden move toward Mona.

Like lightning, Robert grabbed Mr. Montrose and swung him around like a top. He seized Mr.

Montrose's coat lapels, pulling the man eyeball to eyeball. "You weren't thinking of doing anything stupid, were you, Mr. Montrose, because if you were, I would have to interfere, and you don't want me to interfere. Would you, Mr. Montrose?"

Letting loose of Mr. Montrose's lapels, Robert brushed them back into place. "You go with my wife's lads and retire to your home. Have a nice dinner with your wife and tuck the kiddies into bed. Read a good mystery novel. My wife will telephone you when she's ready to meet with you. Now, there's a good gentleman." Robert pushed Montrose toward the Pinkerton guards.

Montrose glanced at Bannock, looking defeated and somewhat stunned by the turn of events. Their plans to control Mona had gone up in smoke.

Pinkertons grabbed each man by the elbow, leading them out through the back of the store and into a car. Mona flipped the OPEN sign CLOSED and locked the front door with keys taken from Otto.

"Now what?" Robert asked, unwrapping a piece of taffy and popping it into his mouth.

"You go to the community center to make

sure the tea setup is going smoothly. I'm going to find Dr. Driscoll and speak with him."

"Take one of the lads with you, Mona."

Mona looked at her watch. "The tea is in two hours. I'll be back long before then. Just make sure everything is ready and don't eat all the tiny sandwiches, my love." She reached up and kissed Robert's cheek before they sauntered out the back door. Robert locked it, handing the keys back to her. They walked together until the path split. Robert with a guard went one way and Mona with her guard headed another.

Mona knew from Rupert that Dr. Driscoll had not left yet. She only hoped she would find the doctor in a more receptive mood than the last time she saw him.

18

Mona and a Pinkerton man entered Dr. Driscoll's office, announcing their presence. Roaming through the many rooms, they found the man in his private quarters at the back of the building packing a suitcase.

Dr. Driscoll looked up in surprise and drew back in fear with his light-colored eyes casting a frosty pall. "Who are you?"

Mona glanced at the open suitcase lying on the bed. "I'm sorry, Dr. Driscoll. We knocked and called out, but no one answered." She turned to her guard and motioned for him to leave. He quietly closed the bedroom door.

Seeing that Dr. Driscoll was still suspicious, Mona spied a rickety chair in the corner and sat in it. "I wish to speak with you, Dr. Driscoll."

Driscoll threw some socks into his suitcase before facing Mona. "You must be Mona Moon. I heard you were coming today. I was going to ask one of your men for a ride out of this pesthole."

"I'd be more than happy to oblige if that is what you want, Dr. Driscoll."

"Good. Good. Yes, it is what I want."

Mona watched Driscoll fold shirts. "You seem agitated, Doctor."

"You think?"

"Doctor, could you stop packing and speak with me? Please take a breather and sit on the bed. Please."

Reluctantly, Driscoll sat down on the edge of the bed facing Mona. "Listen, I tendered my resignation last month. If Montrose didn't get a replacement, that's your problem."

"Dr. Driscoll, I recognize fear when I see it. You just about had a heart attack when we walked in. Can you please share why you are so skittish?"

"Share with you? Ah, lady, don't play dumb. I'm leaving and I won't tell a soul."

"You won't tell a soul what?"

Driscoll looked intently at Mona. "You seem oddly familiar, but I know we haven't met. It's your voice mostly."

"You actually met me not long ago. I came to see you as Mrs. Maplewood."

Driscoll snapped his fingers. "That's it. So you were spying on me even then."

Mona barked, "Don't be so self-important, Doctor. I didn't even know you existed until I met you."

Driscoll drew back and looked disappointed. "Really? You didn't come to spy on me?"

"I came incognito to inspect the conditions of the mine and Mooncrest Village. That's all. Now I'm back in an official capacity as owner of this enterprise. If I am to make changes that will benefit the mine and the miners, I need to have knowledge. Tell me what you know, Dr. Driscoll."

Driscoll pushed back his brown hair which had flopped onto his brow. Reaching into a pocket of his suitcase, he pulled out letters and thrust them at Mona. "Here you go."

Mona gingerly took them and pulled letters out of the envelopes. She read letter after letter.

"Good lord! These are all death threats!"

"Yes, they are."

"Why would you be receiving death threats?"

"I saw too much and made the connections."

Mona encouraged, "Did it have to do with the murder of Piotr Wojcik?"

Driscoll nodded.

"Tell me, sir, all you know."

"I'm a man of science. I believe in facts."

Mona nodded, wishing Driscoll would get to the point.

"I know for a fact that Wheedle did not kill Piotr Wojcik."

"Why is that?"

The doctor stated, "Because I was treating Wheedle for a knife wound at the time Piotr Wojcik was supposedly killed."

Mona leaned back in her chair. "How did Mr. Wheedle get a knife wound?"

Driscoll looked at Mona in disbelief. "From the fight with Wojcik. Don't you know any-thing?"

"Apparently not. You tell me."

"Wojcik picked a fight with Wheedle."

"Over a woman?" Mona asked, seeing if what

Driscoll would tell her matched up with Rupert's report.

"No, it was a personal insult. Wojcik grabbed a religious pouch off Wheedle. To the Indian, that pouch is very personal and powerful medicine. Knives were drawn, and Wheedle was cut on the arm. He came to me for help before he went home. It wasn't a serious wound, but still needed to be cleaned, stitched, and covered with a sterile dressing."

"What about Wojcik?"

"He got cut as well, but I never treated him. The men who witnessed the fight said Wojcik got a ride into town."

"A ride with whom?"

"Otto."

"I see."

"Do you, Miss Moon?"

"Obviously, I don't. Please continue."

Driscoll replied, "Later, one of the miners came to tell me a rumor was going around that Wojcik had been found dead in Butte. I got dressed and commandeered one of the ore trucks and went there."

"Why?"

"Because it is my duty to report on any death with a miner—even if that death occurred off Moon property."

"What happened then?"

"Wojcik's body had been taken to the sheriff's office. A deputy, who I knew was on duty, allowed me to see the body. He owed me a favor. It was Wojcik all right, but he didn't die from a knife wound. He was garroted."

Mona felt faint. "Garroted! Are you sure?"

Driscoll pulled himself up. "I ought to know when a man's head is almost severed."

Disturbed, Mona asked, "Where did this story that Wojcik was knifed in the ribs come from?"

"I don't know, but I read it in the papers and that Wheedle had been arrested. I went to the sheriff and told him that I had been with Wheedle during the time of the murder. Made no difference. I was told to mind my own business. I then asked why the newspaper story reported Wojcik was knifed when he had been garroted. It was made very clear to me that I'd best keep my mouth shut if I wanted to stay healthy. It was a few days later when I started receiving these death threats."

Mona asked, "What is your theory about Wojcik's murder?"

"I deal with facts—not theories."

"If you are a true scientist, then you must have a hypothesis."

Driscoll thought for a moment before answering. "I think Wojcik deliberately attacked Wheedle to cause a disturbance that might snowball into a strike. Then Wojcik was killed to keep him silent when the plan fell through."

"You think he was paid?"

"Yes, ma'am."

"Any ideas who?"

"Take your pick—competing mines, the IWW, disgruntled managers, miners who want to push out Indians and any foreign-born miners."

"Is that everything?"

Driscoll nodded his head.

"I have a question for you, Dr. Driscoll. Why did you say you were waiting for the snow to clear before leaving? You could have left at any time."

Driscoll cleared his throat before answering. "Most of these people can't leave the village until the roads are cleared. They don't have transportation unless they commandeer a truck. I just couldn't leave them in the lurch, but the road is passable now. The miners are free to seek medical attention with the doctor in the next town or Butte, and I am free to leave as well."

"Would you be willing to testify in court, Dr. Driscoll?"

The doctor thought for a moment. "I want to do the right thing, but I also don't want to end up like Wojcik. I would testify only if I am protected. I think whoever sent those death threats was serious."

Mona stood. "I am sorry to lose you, Dr. Driscoll, but I will take you into town. I should be leaving around three-thirty. We shall talk further in Butte. I'll put you on the same hotel floor as me. It's guarded. You'll be safe there."

"I'll be waiting at the store."

"Come to the community center. That's where I'll be." She handed the letters to Driscoll, who put them back in his suitcase.

"All right."

"Until then." Mona stood to leave.

Dr. Driscoll rushed to open the bedroom door for Mona. "See you at three-thirty."

Mona nodded and joined the guard waiting in the hall. She was very upset with what the doctor had related, but was careful not to show it. The threat to the mine was more serious than she had imagined. All the facts pointed to a conspiracy which included Butte's law enforcement.

But why target the Moon Mine and not others?

What did Moon Enterprises own that others wanted and would kill to get?

19

At two o'clock, a few women trickled into the community center to discover tables covered in fine linen tablecloths with matching napkins set with fresh floral centerpieces and gold rimmed white china place settings. Several tables near the stage were set with matching dessert plates with slices of vanilla cake covered in thick vanilla butter icing, lemon bars, sour cream raisin bars, apple-walnut cake with a cinnamon glaze, apple cornbread crisp, sweet potato cakes, molasses cookies, lavender cookies, slab sponge cake, and chocolate-covered sourdough donuts. Dainty bread and butter, cucumber and cream cheese, and roast beef finger sandwiches on soft white bread with the crusts cut off accompanied the desserts. Fruit juice punch, hot tea, coffee, and water were ready to be poured by four waitresses dressed in pink uniforms with starched white aprons standing at attention.

Upon seeing the food, several ladies ran out of the center and down the hill, pounding on the doors of neighbors. "Put on your best frock and come. You've got to see this," the ladies told their friends.

By two-fifteen, thirty-five women were mingling and eagerly chatting up a storm. Since many had never been to a tea before, the waitresses seated them. Women, worn down by the depression and harsh conditions in Mooncrest Village, became quiet when the powdered and rouged waitresses smelling of rose water poured water and punch for them. It had been a long time since anyone had waited upon them or paid any attention to their comfort.

Mona entered the stage dressed in a pink flowered print chiffon dress with matching pink shoes and wearing white gloves. The crowd immediately stopped chatting, looking inquisitively at Mona.

Mona lifted her chin and showed a brave face. "Good afternoon, ladies. I am Mona Moon."

The room remained quiet, but Mona could feel the resentment rising from the audience. "I hope you are enjoying your tea today. I hope to make this an annual event."

Mona was about to utter another announcement when three Blackfoot women entered the center dressed in their finest ceremonial dresses. They stopped and stared at the women who had turned around in their seats to glare at them.

Sensing the tension in the room, Violet showed them to an empty table.

Mona continued, "I welcome you to the first annual tea for the women of Moon Mine."

There was minor applause while three women walked out in protest of the Blackfoot women attending.

Knowing she was getting off to a rocky start, Mona dove into the reason for the tea. "I need your help, ladies. I've gotten reports about things not being quite desirable in Mooncrest Village."

"YOU GOT THAT RIGHT, SISTER!" a woman called out as a murmur spread throughout the room.

Some women laughed while others shushed. "Let Miss Moon speak."

Mona held up her hands. "Like I said—I need your help. Beside your plate, you will find a pencil and a pad with five lines numbered. Put down your suggestions for making Mooncrest Village a better place to live."

"WHAT ABOUT A PROPER STOVE?" the same woman yelled.

Mona smiled. "Write it down as your number one suggestion. This is your time to have a say. Now after the tea, the pads will be collected, and I will review them personally. I do want to mention as of this morning, Otto was relieved as manager for the village store."

There was a scattering of clapping as the women turned to each other, nodding and clucking in approval. Maybe things were changing for the better in the village.

Mona explained, "This is the first of many changes that will be made at Mooncrest Village. I plan to establish more improvements as time and money permit, but I need to have a plan of what needs to be done first. You ladies are to help me. Those who can read and write English, please help those who can't. I just wanted to introduce myself and invite your suggestions. Eat, drink, and be merry. Thank you for coming today. Mona stepped down from the stage and visited tables to shake hands. It wasn't much of a speech she had given, but it broke the ice. Many of the ladies even returned Mona's smile as she shook their hands and learned their names.

She came to a table with a familiar face. "Hello, Miss Tessie."

Startled, Tessie glanced up from writing on her pad. Seeing it was Mona Moon, Tessie stood up from the table. "Hello. Excuse me, but how did you know my name?" She looked curiously at Mona. The woman seemed familiar, but Tessie couldn't quite place her.

"How could I forget the name of a woman who made a buttermilk pie for me?"

Tessie's eyes opened wide and her mouth formed an O. "Bless my soul! It's Mrs. Maplewood. It is, isn't it?" She gave Mona a tight hug and kissed her on both cheeks.

Laughing, Mona returned her hug, saying, "I was undercover. I had to see for myself. It wasn't meant to deceive you personally."

"I had no idea. So, you are not Rupert's cousin from Alabama?"

Mona gave a shy grin and shook her head.

"You are a real duchess? Your husband is from England?"

"Only recently."

"And to think I fed you off a tin plate. I'm so embarrassed," Tessie said, her face blushing.

"I will eat off your tin plates anytime, Miss Tessie. It's the company that's important."

"There you go again calling me Miss Tessie like I was somebody."

"You are to me," Mona said, clasping Tessie's hands. "Now, please excuse me. I must make the rounds, but I want to talk to you later."

Immediately, the tale of Mona inspecting the camp in disguise a short time before spread among the women. They became more receptive to Mona as the tale of her visit disguised as Mrs. Maplewood spread.

Mona finally came to the table where the Blackfoot women sat. "Mrs. Wheedle, thank you for coming. Can you introduce me to your friends?"

"This is Cassie Wheedle and Miriam Wheedle."

Mona raised an eyebrow at the names, but did

not comment. "I find your outfits beautiful. The shells and beading really add to the festivity of the skirts. I know it took hours of work."

"I did not know if we would be welcomed, but I needed to speak with you."

"On behalf of your cousin?"

"He is my husband's cousin, but my husband did not think it proper to speak with you himself as you are married."

"I see. What is it you wish to tell me, Mrs. Wheedle?"

"Can you do something to help him? He is innocent."

"The only thing I can tell you is that we are looking into it. I just talked with Dr. Driscoll who told me he was with your husband's cousin when Wojcik was murdered."

"He plans to tell the sheriff?"

"Dr. Driscoll is willing to testify," Mona said. "That's all I can promise at the moment."

"Do not let an innocent man hang for Wojcik's murder."

Mona clasped Mrs. Wheedle's hand. "I can't promise anything except we will do our best to provide testimony that hopefully will clear your husband's cousin."

"You are the woman who gave us a pie and bread?"

Mona laughed. "How did you recognize me?"

"The voice. You sound like tinkling bells in a breeze."

"That's sweet to say."

"I wish you to have this." Mrs. Wheedle handed a beaded belt to Mona.

"This must have taken much work," Mona said, admiring the belt with beaded images of moose, elk, and bear.

"I won't forget you giving us your bread and pie."

"This belt is worth far more than bread and pie, Mrs. Wheedle, but I accept with thanks. I will treasure this belt always."

Mrs. Wheedle nodded and turned to her relatives. Seeing their message had been delivered, the three Blackfoot women left the center and closed the double doors without making a sound.

One of the other women, seated nearby, muttered, "Good riddance."

Mona caught Violet's concerned stare from across the room. She realized Rupert was right in that she could force the miners to obey the law, but she had little influence over deeply ingrained prejudices. She glanced about the room.

Eastern European women congregated by themselves at one table as black women sat with other women of color, and white women from the South sat together. Only Tessie and a few other women went from table to table assisting women to write down their suggestions. At least, they were all sitting in the same room and seemed to be getting along. Mona discreetly tugged her earlobe signaling for Violet to soldier on. Giving a slight nod, Violet went back to helping the ladies while Mona moved on to the next table greeting her guests. The next time she looked at her watch, the time was three-thirty—time for the tea to end. Mona went to the stage, thanking the women for coming and wishing them a good afternoon as Violet collected the pads from the tables. Promising to notify them of the results, Mona bade them goodbye.

The miners' wives seemed reluctant to leave but bowls of fruit were set outside on the porch as an inducement to leave. The women seeing a chance to snag an orange, a bag of walnuts, or an apple for their children quickly made their way outside. After the last guest departed, the door was locked and the blinds pulled down.

Seeing the waitresses clearing the tables, Mona went over and asked them to pack the leftovers into cardboard lunch boxes for fourteen Pinkerton men and six boxes for herself, Robert, Violet, Rupert, Dexter, and Dr. Driscoll. Violet produced twenty-five thermoses from a box under the table and poured the remaining hot tea, coffee, and punch into them.

Even after the waitresses quickly packed lunch boxes full of goodies and tied them with string, there was still food on the table. Mona requested them to sit and have something to eat before finishing. As the waitresses were relaxing, Mona gave them each a five-dollar bill.

"We've been paid, Miss Moon," one of the waitresses replied, pushing the five dollars away.

"I realize that, but you all made this tea seamless with your cheerful banter and considerate service. Consider this a tip."

The waitress grinned and snatched the bill. "Then I'll take it." She held the bill up to the light and kissed it, saying, "Come to mama, baby," before tucking it between her ample bosom.

Everyone laughed including Mona. She knew how hard these women worked. A little more than two years ago, she was one of these working girls beating around New York City for a job. Five dollars would go a long way.

The laughter was cut short when five Pinkerton men walked into the building from the back. The waitresses immediately sat up straight and pulled down their skirts.

"Miss Moon, we're waiting," one of them said.

"Yes, I know we're behind schedule." Mona turned to the waitresses. "These men will help you clean up and take you back to Butte. Please feel free to take home any food left over. I must take my leave now."

The waitresses stood, saying goodbye.

Mona and Violet had two of the Pinkerton men carry out the lunch boxes and thermoses to the waiting touring car where the rest of the Pinkertons, Rupert, Robert with Chloe, and Dexter stood waiting. Violet handed out the boxes and thermoses to each man.

Robert immediately opened his and stuffed a roast beef sandwich into his mouth. "I'm starving. How did the tea go?"

"Robert, don't talk with your mouth full," Mona admonished.

"One of your wifely duties is to make sure I'm fed."

"That's what cooks are for."

"Well? How did it go?" Robert asked, shrugging off Chloe who wanted some of the sandwich.

"I think it went fine. Actually, better than I thought it would." Mona reached into the box and pulled out another roast beef sandwich for Chloe.

Dexter pointed to his wristwatch. "We need to go, Mona."

Mona looked around. "Where is Dr. Driscoll? He wanted to leave with us."

Exasperated, Rupert said, "I'll fetch him." Rupert tucked his thermos in his coat pocket and box under his arm, not trusting the Pinkerton men to refrain from filching his food.

The Pinkertons good-naturedly ribbed Rupert as he walked toward the medical building.

"Let's wait inside the car," Violet suggested. "It's cold."

Mona said, "You go ahead, Violet. I want

some fresh air."

Violet, Dexter, and the driver got inside the warm vehicle.

Ten minutes went by as Mona and Robert stood waiting along with the rest of the Pinkerton men. Mona wished Rupert and Dr. Driscoll would hurry.

"Let's drive to the man's office," Robert suggested.

"He didn't want to be seen with us. That's why we're waiting at the back of the center."

Suddenly they heard Rupert shouting and running toward them. Mona and Robert rushed to meet him with the Pinkertons following. Upon seeing the knot of people, Rupert fell to his knees breathing heavily.

"What's the matter?" Mona asked. She had a bad feeling as Rupert almost never panicked.

Robert pulled Rupert to his feet. He, too, was shocked at seeing Rupert so discombobulated. "What is it, man? Pull yourself together!"

Rupert sputtered, "Dr. Driscoll is dead! He's hanging from a tree outside his office!"

20

Mona, Robert, Rupert, and six of the Pinkertons rushed to the doctor's office. They came upon Dr. Driscoll's limp body suspended from a limb swaying in the gentle breeze on the west side of the building near a stand of alder trees. The man's eyes bulged from their sockets and his tongue had blackened.

Mona gave a small cry and for a moment covered her eyes with her hands.

"Mona, go back. I'll take care of this," Robert ordered.

Lowering her hands, Mona shook her head. "No, love, I'll be all right. It's such a shock. Driscoll told me he feared for his life. I never dreamed any harm would come to him with us here. I failed him, Robert. I shan't fail him now."

A Pinkerton climbed the tree to cut Driscoll down.

"Stop!" Mona insisted. "Don't touch the body. Everyone, quit moving about." She pointed to one of the Pinkertons. "You there. Take Rupert's truck and get the sheriff."

"Yes, ma'am."

Mona asked, "Does anyone have a camera?"

Rupert answered, "There's one in the store. I'll get it."

Mona handed him the key. "Bring lanterns back. It will be getting dark soon. Tell Dexter to come here, but have the driver take Violet back to the hotel. I don't want her to see this, Rupert."

"Will do."

"Have four of the Pinkertons blockade the road. None of the miners are to leave Mooncrest Village. Oh, Rupert, there are the waitresses still cleaning up. Not a word to them about this and have them leave as soon as possible. They don't need to be involved."

Rupert nodded and left with a Pinkerton to carry out Mona's orders.

Twenty minutes later, Dexter and Rupert came back carrying boxes with flashlights, lanterns, and a Leica 35 mm camera. Rupert said, "I sent the waitresses home, saying we'd finish cleaning up. Violet's on her way back to the hotel as well. I didn't tell her about this. Just said Dr. Driscoll was ill, and we would follow later."

Dexter stood by Robert, staring at the late doctor. "This is a hell of a thing."

Mona asked Rupert, "You know how to use the camera?"

A Pinkerton stepped forward. "I do, Miss Moon. I was trained to take crime scene photographs."

"Then do so. I want close-ups of Driscoll's hands, any signs of a struggle—that type of thing. When you finish with the body, come to the medical office. We'll take more photographs."

Another Pinkerton asked, "Should we cut him down after the photographs?"

Mona answered, "No, let the sheriff do that. We don't want to be accused of tampering with the crime scene. One more thing, gentlemen, when the sheriff comes, no one is to tell him that we took photographs. Understood?"

The men murmured, "Yes."

"Good. Now pass the word along."

"My, you are a cool customer, Mona," Robert said, admiring his wife.

"He's not the first murdered human I've come across," Mona replied. She wanted to collapse in Robert's arms; however, the current situation demanded cunning, action, and strong leadership. She would have the luxury of falling apart tonight, but now she must act swiftly. There was very limited time before the law arrived.

"Dexter, you stay here and act as a witness that nothing was tampered with. However, you might want to check Dr. Driscoll's pockets. There might be something in them like a note."

"I will, Mona. Where will you be?"

"Robert and I are going to check Dr. Driscoll's office. Send the photographer to me when he's finished here."

"What do you want of me?" Rupert asked, tagging after Mona and Robert.

Mona said, "Come with us. I need you to check the office to see if anything is missing."

All three wrapped their coats tighter around them as they trudged through the snow into office. Upon entering the building, Mona switched on the lights.

"It's so cold in here," Mona said, shivering.

"There is no one to feed the stoves," Rupert answered, looking inside the recovery room to see if there were any patients.

Mona looked for clues in the long hallway going back to the doctor's private living quarters. She opened the door to his bedroom. "Don't touch anything if you're not wearing gloves."

"We are, Mona," Robert assured. "What are you looking for?"

"Where is Dr. Driscoll's suitcase? He was packing to leave."

Rupert pulled back the curtain on the closet. "Here it is." He placed the suitcase on the bed and opened it. "Empty."

"Check the pockets. Driscoll had stashed some letters in the pockets."

Rupert reached into the various pockets of the suitcase. "Nothing."

"Looks like someone has stolen them, Mona," Robert said.

Rupert asked, "What kind of letters were they?"

"Death threats. That's why Driscoll wanted to leave. He was afraid for his life. If only I had put a guard on him," Mona ruminated. "So stupid of me."

Rupert put the suitcase back. "Who would dare do such a thing as to murder the doc with all of us here? Boggles the mind at the daring."

Mona went to the dresser and pulled on the drawers. "His clothes have been put back." She went into the doctor's bathroom and saw that his toiletries were replaced in the medicine cabinet.

Robert and Rupert followed Mona into the office. All three of them stared at an unsealed envelope on the desk with a generous scrawl across the front. It was addressed to—Mrs. Mona Moon Farley.

Mona picked up the envelope.

"Wait a minute, Mona," Robert cautioned. "That's evidence."

"It's addressed to me. I'm going to read it." She pulled out the letter and held it up for all three to read.

Miss Moon, I can't go on. This is the best way. My apologies.

Gene Driscoll

"Someone is trying to make Driscoll's death

appear to be a suicide," Mona complained.

Rupert asked, "Could it have been a suicide?"

"No way. The man wanted to live. He did not die by his own hand," Mona said, putting the letter in her pocket.

"Mona, are you sure you are doing the right thing by taking that letter?" Robert asked.

"I am not going to have Driscoll's death labeled a suicide. Let's see if the sheriff asks if we found anything in the office," Mona said.

There was a knock on the office door. Startled, all three looked up to see the Pinkerton holding the camera. "All done outside, ma'am."

"Take pictures of the bedroom, bathroom, and office please. I want even the contents of the closet, medicine cabinet, and dresser photographed."

"I understand."

"When you are finished, put the camera back in the store. Is there someone we can trust developing the film? I don't dare have photographs made in Butte."

"There is a retired agent in Billings who is an amateur photographer. He has a darkroom and will help us," the Pinkerton answered.

Mona ordered, "Get a couple of mates and take one of the cars. Drive through the night if you must, but get that film developed. You understand no one must know you have the film on you."

"We'll get 'er done, ma'am. We're Pinkerton men."

If Mona hadn't felt so guilty over Dr. Driscoll's death, she would have smiled at the man's bravado. Instead, she felt nauseous. Mona rushed out of the building, holding a hand to her mouth.

How could such a triumphant day have descended into this meaningless tragedy?

21

Mona spent the next day in bed.

Dexter ran interference with the sheriff wanting to question her, saying the hotel doctor had prescribed tranquilizers for her distraught nerves after seeing so horrible a sight of Dr. Driscoll swinging lifeless from a tree. The sheriff could do nothing but wait for Mona to recover.

Meanwhile, Mona went down the Hotel Finlen's hallway of her rented floor and knocked on a door. A Pinkerton man answered and let her inside. The blinds were pulled down keeping out the morning sun, and only a few lamps were on, giving the room a ghostly pall. On the bed, Otto lay gagged and trussed up like a roped calf in a rodeo.

Another Pinkerton entered the room and

stood by the door while a man guarded the window. In total there were three Pinkerton men in the room with Mona and Otto. Dexter entered the room a moment later.

Mona pulled a chair next to the bed. "Ungag him."

A Pinkerton untied the gag.

Otto immediately screamed, "HELP! HELP! SOMEONE HELP ME!"

A Pinkerton brandished a slapjack causing Otto to quit yelling.

Mona straightened her skirt before studying Otto. "There's no use shouting. No one can hear you."

"The people on the floor below this room can. They'll tell the manager," Otto said.

Mona shook her head. "I've rented those rooms and this entire floor. Believe me when I say no one can hear you but us."

Otto looked deflated. "This is kidnapping. What do you want with me?"

"Do you recognize me?"

"You're Mona Moon."

"Yes, but you first met me as Mrs. Maplewood, Rupert Hunt's cousin, from Alabama."

As recognition dawned, Otto's face drained of color, leaving his bulbous nose looking as red as a Christmas tree bulb.

Mona continued, "You sold me clothes from the Mooncrest Village store at outrageous prices. Remember?"

Otto gulped. "We must price items to their real cost which included scarcity, transportation, and incidentals."

"You charged me a month's wages for items worth no more than twenty dollars at the most."

Otto licked his lips. "My throat is dry. May I have a glass of water?"

A Pinkerton handed him a paper cup filled with cool water.

Otto drank it and then said, "I can explain the high prices, Miss Moon."

"I can explain it also, Otto." Mona pulled out two sets of accounting ledgers from the satchel Dexter had brought into the room.

Upon seeing the ledgers, Otto winced, emitting a low moan.

"Yes, we found the real ledgers, Otto, in the outhouse under one of the portals, which is one of the reasons I am wearing gloves right now.

Thank you for at least putting the ledgers in a leather briefcase."

"I've never seen those ledgers before."

"But the handwriting is yours. I've already had a handwriting expert from Helena look at samples of your handwriting and will testify in court that both ledgers were written by you. I also hired two accountants from San Francisco. They will arrive this afternoon and pick these books clean."

Otto swung his head back and forth between Mona and the Pinkertons, looking for an avenue of escape.

"We'll get back to the ledgers in a moment. I want to know about Piotr Wojcik."

"What about him?"

Mona asked, "What did you have to do with the man's death?"

"Ah, no. Ah, no! You're not gonna pin that murder on me. It was Wheedle who killed Wojcik."

"No, he didn't. Dr. Driscoll told me that he was treating Wheedle's knife injury at the time of Wojcik's murder. Wheedle never went into Butte like Wojcik did."

"He's lying."

"What reason would Dr. Driscoll lie about such a thing? However, I saw how you treated that Indian couple wanting to purchase food in the store. I think your hatred of Indians might include you as a suspect. Where were you the night of the murder?"

"If I am a racist as you say, then I would have killed Wheedle—not Wojcik."

"Where were you that night?"

"Since my gig with the Moon Mines is up, I'll tell you what I was doing. I was selling bootleg whiskey out of the back of the store. I can get fifteen men to vouch for me as I sold the last bottle around eleven. I didn't have time to go into Butte and kill Wojcik."

"You drove Wojcik into Butte. I have witnesses."

"Yeah. I had to make a run to Butte for more whiskey. I let Wojcik off in Butte, met with my bootleg supplier, and went back to Mooncrest Village. I have men who will testify what time they bought whiskey from me."

"Do you know who killed Wojcik?"

"NO!"

Mona turned to Dexter who was furiously taking notes. "Can you have you-know-who check into this man's story?"

Dexter paused writing. "You betcha. Shouldn't be too hard to confirm as soon as Otto gives us the men's names. Until the story is assessed, let's continue with the embezzlement issue."

Crossing her legs and shifting in her seat, Mona demanded, "What I want is the name of the man who was your partner in this embezzlement scheme. We have you selling illegal whiskey and cheating Moon Enterprises. I will cut a deal if you give me all you know."

"What kind of a deal?"

"I want names of everyone involved. Then I want gossip, rumors, and outright threats from any miner or his family."

Sweat beaded on Otto's forehead. "There was no one else. It was all me. I confess."

"All right then. Have it your way." She ordered the Pinkertons, "Clean the man up and let him go."

A Pinkerton unsheathed a switchblade and cut Otto's bindings.

Otto hurriedly shook off the ropes tying him. "I'm going to the sheriff and order your arrest for kidnapping," Otto warned.

Unimpressed by Otto's threat, Mona said, "One more thing, Otto. I need to tell you that Doctor Driscoll was found dead yesterday swinging from a tree. Now we both know he didn't commit suicide."

Otto seemed panicky, sitting on the side of the bed. "The doctor is really dead?"

"Quite dead, I'm sorry to say."

Otto pleaded, "Look. I can't be seen in this hotel. There are too many spies in the lobby and amongst the staff. I'm sure no one recognized me yesterday because your men pulled my hat brim down over my face as we came up the back stairs."

"That won't happen today. My men are going to escort you down the elevator and out through the lobby in the full light of day. Everyone will see you. I'm going to throw you to the wolves."

Otto protested, "I didn't reveal a thing."

"No one will believe you didn't snitch. Also, I had one of my men deposit five hundred dollars into your bank account this morning. Won't that set tongues wagging?”

"You didn't!”

"I did." Mona turned to leave.

"WAIT!" Otto hung his head in shame and fear. "I'll tell you everything I know. Just don't hang me out to dry."

"I think *hang* is the operative word here," Mona replied.

"I bet the real story is a doozy," Dexter murmured.

And it was!

22

Mona and Robert spent the rest of the day in their suite while Dexter Deatherage and Rupert Hunt listened to Otto's tale of greed, deception, and theft, which was also recorded on Dictaphone wax cylinders. At five o'clock they knocked on Mona's suite.

Violet opened the door, saying, "Just in time for tea, gentlemen."

Chloe pranced excitedly around the room, jumping on the furniture.

"Get down, Chloe," Violet admonished, as she beckoned the men to sit.

"Is Mona here?" Dexter asked. "I want to deliver my report."

Mona entered the drawing room from her suite. "I'm here, Dexter. I heard your knock."

Robert followed and clapped his hands together with enthusiasm. "Good, Violet. You've ordered tea." He immediately sat down and filled a plate with sandwiches and slices of candied fruit cake.

Ignoring her famished husband, Mona took a seat opposite Dexter and Rupert. "What's the gist?"

Dexter explained, "I have a signed confession to the embezzlement and a signed affidavit to the entire sordid ordeal. We have Otto lock, stock, and barrel."

"Can he recant?" Mona asked, pouring tea into cups and handing them around.

"Of course, he can try, but we have the second set of accounting books in his handwriting with a witness account of being over-charged, and his signed confession plus the Dictaphone cylinders. As a notary and an officer of the courts, I certified the documents so they will be admissible in court. There is also the matter of five hundred dollars dropped into his account."

"What about the Pinkerton who deposited the money?"

Dexter said, "The bills were from a Helena

bank, and we made sure the serial numbers were non-sequential. The Pinkerton has left town. There is no way the deposit will be traced back to us."

"Where is Otto now?" Robert asked.

"Tucked away in a safe house with two of our men."

Robert looked up from drinking his tea. "We have a safe house?"

Mona looked surprised and shrugged, "I guess we do now."

"You have an appointment with the sheriff at ten tomorrow," Dexter said, looking at his appointment book.

"We shall be there," Robert said.

Dexter shook his head, "You're not going, Robert."

Robert's eyebrows drew together. "Why bloody not?"

"Because you have a temper, especially where Mona is concerned. Also, you going to the office will hit the papers. Let's not give reporters more fodder than they already have. Since the sheriff is asking for Mona, that's who will be going."

Robert huffed, "I don't see why you can't take

a statement from Mona at the hotel and be done."

"This is a game, Robert. The sheriff wants to know what we know, and the questions he asks will give us insight into the evidence he has," Dexter explained.

"What am I supposed to do? Sit here and twiddle my thumbs while my wife is being interrogated?"

"You are going to take care of this for us, Robert," Mona said, handing him an envelope.

"What's this?" Robert said, opening it.

"It's an invitation from Margaret Daly. We are invited to a square dance tomorrow night at her home estate called Riverside."

"Who's Margaret Daly?" Violet asked, peeking at the engraved invitation.

Dexter answered, "One of the richest women in America. Her husband, Marcus Daly owned the Anaconda Mine of which she still has a major interest. He is considered one of the three copper kings."

Robert looked up from the invitation. "This reads more like a summons."

Mona nodded. "That's the impression I got as well."

"Do you think it is a trap?"

"Let's go and find out, Robert."

He grinned. "I'm game, darling. Better than sitting around this dull hotel."

Violet said, "It says to wear Western or historical pioneer clothing. It's a theme party."

"Violet, can you whip up something for us to wear?" Mona asked.

"Of course. I'm bored myself. Will be happy to have something to do beside take Chloe on walks."

"What is a square dance?" Robert asked, rubbing his chin.

"Something similar to English folk dances but with a live caller," Mona said upon seeing Robert's confusion.

"What's a live caller?"

Mona said, "A person who tells the dancers what steps to take. Call to motion in other words."

Robert asked, "Do you know how to square dance, Mona?"

Mona laughed. "Haven't a clue."

"We'll have to fake it then," Robert gleefully announced, handing the invitation to Violet.

"And see what Margaret Daly has in store for us," Mona agreed.

Dexter tapped on his teacup with a spoon. "Right now, I need to prep Mona for her interview with the sheriff, so please excuse us." Dexter rose and motioned for Mona to follow him.

Mona caught a last glimpse at Robert who stuck his tongue out at her while crossing his eyes.

She returned the gesture, satisfied Robert still had her back.

It wasn't the honeymoon Mona had dreamed of, but as long as Robert was with her, she was content.

Let the world do its worst.

23

Mona looked every inch a powerful woman when she entered the sheriff's office dressed in a white woolen dress and matching coat hitting mid-calf with white gloves, pale beige boots, and a cloche hat accenting her platinum hair. Taking off her sunglasses, she placed them in her white purse.

Even though the sheriff and his men knew about Mona's amber eyes, they couldn't help being surprised at seeing them. Mona returned their curious stare, causing the men to shy away.

Mona was shown the best chair in the office where she gave a detailed account of the day's events and the discovery of Dr. Driscoll. After hearing Mona's story, the sheriff began shooting questions at her and Dexter, who had accompanied her.

"Is it your opinion Dr. Driscoll took his own life?" the sheriff asked, perched on the edge of his desk, poised over Mona. He was difficult to see as the window light shone behind him.

Mona answered distinctly, "I think Dr. Driscoll was murdered as he had shown me death threat letters shortly before his death. He literally begged me to drive him into Butte."

A stenographer quietly took notes in the corner.

"You say you witnessed the doctor packing a suitcase, but we found nothing packed, and his suitcase was stashed in the closet. We certainly didn't find any death threats."

Mona answered, "That was because his murderer or murderers were smart enough to unpack his things and put them away. I will not agree with you that his death was a suicide because I know it was not."

"Then how do you explain this, Miss Moon." The sheriff handed Mona a typed letter. "This was found on Dr. Driscoll's desk."

Mona unfolded the letter and read. It was a typed letter from Dr. Driscoll stating that he was going to hang himself. Disgusted, she tossed the letter back, as she knew the letter was a fake and had been planted. Mona didn't disclose that she had stolen the original fake suicide note, as she was positive the doctor had been murdered. She asked, "Have you had the signature identified by a handwriting expert as Dr. Driscoll's handwriting and have you tracked down the typewriter?"

Dexter sat stone-faced, surprised at the appearance of a second "suicide" note, keeping his knowledge of the first note under his hat. He had been against Mona taking the first letter, but now knew Mona was right about the cause of Driscoll's death. It had been murder or how else could a second "suicide" note appear?

"The typewriter was found in his office. Now this letter closes the case."

Mona was insistent. "I think it is easy enough to establish the signature is not Dr. Driscoll's. If you go public with the statement that Dr. Driscoll committed suicide, I will tell the newspapers I do not agree with your assessment."

"Why would anyone want to kill the doc?"

"Because he knew Wheedle was innocent of killing Piotr Wojcik. He was treating the man in Mooncrest Village while Wojcik was murdered in

Butte. He told you of this, and you ignored his account. Doesn't look good for your department when an outstanding member of the community has testimony to set a man free and is ignored. On top of that, the witness shows up dead. It casts suspicion on you and your men."

The sheriff, trying to be intimidating, slid off the corner of his desk and faced Mona. "I don't like threats, Miss Moon."

"Nor do I, Sheriff. I know for a fact there was no suicide note left on that desk before your men arrived. I had pictures taken of the body and the medical building. A picture was taken specifically of the desk. There was no letter," Mona lied.

The sheriff's eyes widened as he tipped back the Stetson on his head. "I need those pictures and the negatives."

Dexter intervened. "We will have a set of pictures sent to you, Sheriff. We want to cooperate in every way."

"I want the negatives as well."

"We can't oblige. The negatives are the property of Moon Enterprises," Dexter said, keeping a friendly tone.

"Then I'll get a court order and have you two

arrested for interfering with my investigation."

Dexter shot back. "Go right ahead, but we will release the pictures to the newspapers before you get your court order, and we will tie you up in court for years over it. As for arresting Miss Moon and myself for interfering, we will sue you personally for malfeasance. Besides, I don't think the governor of Montana would appreciate such treatment of Miss Moon since she is one of the largest employers and taxpayers in the state. She is attending a party at Riverside tonight, and I believe the governor will be in attendance."

The lawman sank back on his desk, knowing he had been bested.

Mona said, "This is what I want for Dr. Driscoll. I'm going to send my own pathologist to do an autopsy. Then I want his death investigated as a murder and an investigation into who placed the typewritten suicide letter on the man's desk."

Rising from his chair, Dexter said, "I think we are finished. One more thing, Sheriff. Have your men quit following Miss Moon and anyone in the Moon-Farley party. They have been shadowing us since we hit this burg." He crooked his arm for Mona. "Come, Miss Moon. We are done here."

Mona took Dexter's arm and they left the building.

As soon as they entered their waiting car, Mona asked, "How do you think that went?"

"It was rougher than I thought it would be. The sheriff was very combative when you didn't roll over at his suggestion of suicide. What's your take on this entire mess, Mona?"

"I think several people from our employee pool are working with outside forces to foment a major strike at Moon Mine. I say *our people* because they sneaked right past our Pinkertons to kill the doctor in broad daylight with us not more than five hundred feet away. I also say *our people* and not person because Dr. Driscoll was a big man. It would take more than one person to take him down and string him up. They would have worked fast because people were out and about."

Dexter observed, "The trees around the medical building give cover. It's kind of isolated."

Mona paused for a moment and reached for a hanky inside her purse. "I will regret to my dying day that I did not put a Pinkerton guard over Driscoll. Such a useless death. The man had so much to offer."

"I think we both are sure someone with the sheriff's department planted the second suicide letter and is working with those responsible for both Piotr Wojcik's and Gene Driscoll's murders."

"I agree, Dexter. I can't believe our enemies think they can get away with their tampering."

Dexter replied, "They have, and they've been very effective so far. We need to be careful, Mona. Bluffing on our part can only go so far. Sooner or later, whoever is behind this series of tragedies is going to hit us and hit us hard."

Mona asked, "Don't you believe the sheriff is acting on someone else's orders?"

"If he is involved as we suspect, he must know we have the first suicide letter. He can't accuse us of taking it as it would implicate him. People would ask how the sheriff knew there was a first suicide note. Again, it might not be him, but one of his men involved. We need to have evidence before we accuse anyone. Whoever we are up against, I think their fingers reach deep into Moon Enterprises. All I can say at this juncture is be safe, Mona. You and Robert, be careful because they will come after you both."

"I am going to Riverside tonight. Maybe I'll find some answers there. At least, I plan to speak to the governor."

"I think you and Robert should be packing tonight."

Mona patted her purse which held her snub nose revolver. "I never go anywhere without my little friend. Don't worry, Dexter. Both Robert and I will be fully loaded for bear or *bar* as Daniel Boone would say."

"Just make sure you hit your target as old Daniel did."

Mona patted Dexter reassuringly on the forearm before glancing out the window. For a moment, she daydreamed of being in Venice, dressed in a gossamer blue gown dancing the waltz with Robert. Closing her eyes, she heard the music and actually felt the parquet floor beneath her satin dance slippers. Robert suddenly let go and Mona stumbled backward. As she reached for him, Robert disappeared into a consuming mist. She ran after, but couldn't find him.

Mona shuddered, hoping her daydream was just that—a sick fantasy of her mind and not some foreboding of things to come.

24

Mona and Robert stepped into the brilliantly lit Riverside, home of Margaret Daly. They looked about the Georgian-Revival mansion, which boasted fifty rooms, twenty-five bedrooms, and fifteen bathrooms.

A maid helped with their coats. Robert sported a gunslinger's black outfit with a real loaded gun residing in his holster while Mona wore a cowgirl's red felt skirt sporting fringe, a white blouse with black cuffs, a black belt, black boots, and a red vest to match the skirt. She declined to give her cowgirl hat to the maid as she wanted Robert to spot her anywhere in the mansion.

Mona noticed a man helping another couple with their coats and elbowed Robert in the ribs. "Robert, look. That man. He followed us on the train. Remember?"

Robert gave the man a quick look and whispered back, "How can you be sure without the Stetson?"

"Because he has a milky left eye. The man who followed us had a milky left eye."

"Well, now you know he works for the Anaconda Mine. He's probably snooping through everyone's coat pockets right now. Let's forget about him, darling, and have a good time."

Mona sighed, feeling like she was living in a fishbowl.

They joined the receiving line and soon were face to face with their hostess, Margaret Daly, dressed as saloon madam in a floor-length, purple sequined dress, with ostrich feathers springing from her elaborate, upswept hairdo and a splendid pearl, neck choker. Mrs. Daly shook Mona's hand heartily and said, "I've been wanting to meet you for a long time, Your Grace."

"Please call me Mona."

"Call me Maggie then. My husband always did."

"Very well, then. Thank you for inviting us, Maggie."

Maggie looked admirably at Robert. "My, you're a tall, cool drink of water, Your Grace."

"I'm in the States now, Miss Maggie. Robert will suffice."

Maggie gave a nod of her head before leaning into Mona. "I must talk to you later." She straightened and greeted the next guest in line.

Realizing they had been dismissed, Mona and Robert wandered in search of refreshments. They found a table laden with all sorts of meat—beef, pork, chicken, salmon, even deer and moose venison. Another table was loaded with bite-size food, including an assortment of savory cheese balls, crackers and toasted breads, deviled eggs, hard-boiled eggs, caviar rolls, tomato aspic, sardines, chicken liver in bacon blankets, smoked salmon canapés, cranberry-apple gelatin mold, jellied anchovy molds, radish roses, endive stuffed with cream cheese. Close by was the last table topped with maple meringue rolls, caramel tea rolls, slices of chocolate cake with marshmallow icing, ginger cake squares, and vanilla ice cream.

The champagne flowed freely but Mona and Robert each took a mug of hot spiced cider. They needed their heads to be clear as they sat at one of the tables covered with red and white checkered tablecloths.

It took a long time to finish their plates as guests made a beeline to their table to introduce themselves. They wanted to get a first-hand glimpse of Mona's famed platinum hair and amber eyes, so they could tell their friends they had met the famous duke and duchess. Eager couples inevitably approached the table when Robert and Mona were chewing which made things awkward. Even the governor came over to introduce himself. Mona and Robert stood to exchange pleasantries with him and his wife until the couple excused themselves to dance.

Robert watched the governor do-si-do and promenade with the best of them. "Want to give it a whirl, Mrs. Maplewood?"

Folding her napkin, Mona said, "I'll give it a go if you do."

"I do."

Just as Robert rose to escort Mona to the dance floor, an estate secretary intercepted them and whispered into Mona's ear that Mrs. Daly was waiting in the study. Would Mona please follow?

Mona shrugged at Robert. "Duty calls."

"I'll be right behind you, padnah," Robert said, affecting a western drawl.

The secretary showed Mona the study, but cautioned Robert to wait outside. She gathered a chair for him. Resigned, Robert was content to guard the door.

Mona entered the study and saw Mrs. Daly standing before a roaring blaze. She motioned for Mona to sit on the couch facing the fire.

"You wanted to see me, Maggie?"

The elderly lady sat next to Mona. "This is my favorite room. It was my husband's study. I can still smell his cigars and aftershave lotion when I enter."

"You must miss him very much."

"I do, Mona. You know Marcus died in 1900. I've been a widow for thirty-four years now. Soon, it will be thirty-five years. It's a terrible thing when a wife outlives her husband for so long, but my time to join him is coming soon. I hope such a prison sentence does not await you."

"Why do you say that, Maggie?"

"I can tell you and your husband truly love each other. That's how it was with Marcus and me. It was a love match. It's why I wanted to speak to you in private."

"Go ahead. I'm listening."

"You disrupt people, my dear. Not only is it due to your unusual coloring, but your personal views upset certain people. You are thought of as strange, and those in power have decided you are not one of them; therefore, something to fear."

"These people have spoken to you?"

"They have spoken in front of me, and what they say frightens me. I want to warn you to be careful. Very careful."

"I take it that these men you speak of are my competitors."

"Yes, and they believe they can run you out of business. They're convinced you are a socialist and will allow unions at your mines."

Mona paused for a moment. "Maggie, I'll be frank with you since you are taking a risk warning me. I don't give an owl's hoot whether the miners unionize or not. I would prefer not having to deal with a union, but I understand why the workers want one. One thing I will not abide is the bloodshed that happened at the Anaconda Mine Road massacre in 1920—one man was killed and sixteen men were shot in the back as they fled. I just won't have that kind of violence on my watch."

"Once the unions get in, they will make demands we can't meet. It will eventually shut down the mines."

Mona replied, "That's poppycock. There's enough money in those mines for everyone to get a nice chunk of change, including the owners. Do you really think it's fair for you to live in a fifty-room mansion while the miners live in tar-paper shacks? That's simply not the cowgirl way."

"I don't see you living in a shack yourself. I've seen pictures of Moon Manor. It's quite impressive."

"The difference is I pay my staff a nice living. Look, Maggie, I'm just a working stiff. I know what it is to be without a job, wondering where my next meal was coming from, living without running water, sharing a toilet with dozens of other people. I didn't like it, so if the miners want to collectively bargain, so be it. I'm not going to crack some man's head open over fifteen cents more an hour."

Maggie wore a sour expression. "You're a

little firecracker, Mona. I felt it my Christian duty to warn you, and now I have." She rose.

Mona rose as well and held out her hand. "Let's part friends, Maggie Daly. In fact, I'd love to show you the Bluegrass and Mooncrest Farm this summer."

Maggie shook Mona's hand. "We *are* friends, dear girl. I admire your spunk, and I wish nothing but the best for you and your husband. I must be excused now. My guests are waiting."

She swept out of the study with Mona following her.

Robert gave Mona an inquisitive look.

"Lord Bob, let's give this square dancing a couple of tries and then vamoose. I feel very exposed here."

Robert bowed. "Your wish is my command." He wrapped Mona's arm around his, and they both made their way to the dance floor where they followed the caller's instructions and cut quite a rug.

Within an hour, they were in their car on the way back to their hotel in Butte where Mona related Maggie's warning.

Robert pulled Mona close to him and murmured, "Don't worry, Mona. Everything will be all right. I'll see to it."

The only thing was Robert didn't realize what was about to happen.

25

As Mona and Robert compared notes while riding back to the hotel, both of them heard a loud cracking noise that traveled through the car.

"What was that?" Mona asked. "It sounded like the snap of a bullwhip."

Robert ordered the driver, "Slow down, please." He rolled down his window and listened.

"There it is again," Mona said. "Driver, stop." She got out of the car and looked about, but it was dark with a moonless sky. Mona couldn't see anything.

Another crack sounded.

The Pinkertons in the car following them also got out and looked about.

A fourth crack pierced the air.

"It's gunfire! Take cover," one of the Pinkertons shouted.

Mona ducked down by the side of the car as Robert joined her. "Turn the car lights off!" she yelled.

Robert threw Mona on the ground and shielded her with his body, but they both lifted their heads upon hearing a rumble.

"AVALANCHE! AVALANCHE!" Robert yelled, as he dragged Mona to the side of the mountain and frantically covered both their heads with his arms. Their driver huddled with them. Since darkness prevented them from seeing which direction the snow was headed, there was no use in running. Some of the Pinkertons realized they were in the path of the descending wall of snow and ran. Their shrieks could be heard above the roar of the torrent as they got caught in the avalanche and were hurled down the mountainside.

"Oh, God!" Mona murmured upon hearing the men scream.

Robert whispered into her ear, "Don't listen. Don't listen." He put his hands over her ears.

The rumbling abruptly stopped and was replaced by a haunting silence. Robert and Mona waited a few minutes before climbing out of the snowbank which had fallen about them. Luckily, they had not been hit with any of the displaced rocks and boulders propelled by the tumbling snow. Robert cleared snow from their driver who also was unharmed.

Shouts came from the Pinkertons who had been in a car ahead of them. They had not been involved in the avalanche. "Anyone hurt?" one guard shouted.

Robert yelled, "Second car is fine except we are bound by snow, but the third car got the brunt of the slide. We think there are casualties, but we can't see and no one is answering our calls."

"We are digging you out now. Can you get into your car?"

Robert replied, "Negative. The doors are blocked by snow."

"Stay where you are. We are coming."

Mona, Robert, and the driver helped each other get the snow from around their collars, inside their gloves, and tops of their boots. Each gave a vigorous shake to remove snow from their coats. Both the driver and Robert dug snow away with their hands from the trunk of the car to access a shovel, emergency blankets, and a first-aid kit. Mona moved to the back passenger door and pulled snow away from the car with her hands. The work kept them all warm.

As the Pinkertons in the first car were making headway with the fallen snow, Mona and Robert saw car lights in the distance behind them, curving the bend in the road. They heard the roar of the car engine and saw beams of flashlights.

"HELLO? HELLO?"

Robert shouted, "WE'RE HERE!"

Mona grabbed Robert's arm. "Robert, be careful. These could be the men who caused the avalanche."

"WE'LL HELP YOUR MEN. THE CAR'S GONE OVER THE SIDE."

Robert yelled back, "YES, DO THAT! WE'LL FREE OUR CAR AND THEN START DIGGING TOWARD YOU." Turning, Robert asked, "Do you have your gun on you, Mona?"

"It's in my purse which is in the car. What about your six-shooter?"

"Under the snow somewhere."

"I've got one in my shoulder holster, and there's another gun in the glove compartment if we can get to it," the Pinkerton driver announced.

"Good man," Robert said. "Put your gun where you can use it in a hurry."

Mona, Robert, and the driver dug around their car finally clearing the snow away from the trunk. The driver took the shovel and shoveled the road while Robert put several blankets around Mona, whose hands had frozen so badly that she lost the feeling in them.

After an hour, the Pinkertons from the first car cleared away the snow and reached Mona and Robert. They put Mona in their vehicle which was still warm. She was grateful for the warmth and rubbed her numb hands in front of the car's heater.

Robert worked with the Pinkertons to reach the third car, but once they broke through a wall of snow, there was no third car. It had careened down the mountain. Its blinking tail lights were faintly visible beneath the snow.

They found four men hoisting bodies through a series of ropes tied to a truck. A man wearing a Stetson and standing near the road's edge, watched them bring the bodies up. Upon seeing his milky eye, Robert recognized the man, who worked for Margaret Daly.

Robert walked up to the man. "Is everyone dead?"

"No. I have two men in the truck. They are banged up a bit. They told me that someone repeatedly fired a gun, which caused the avalanche."

"How did you happen upon us?" Robert asked.

"Miss Margaret gave orders to follow. She felt you were in danger although we never expected anything like this. You've got to admit it was devilishly clever."

Not sure the Stetson man was speaking the truth, Robert gave him a long stare before stating, "Thank you. Our other two cars are working, so we'll take the injured men into town and send help back."

"We'll stay and clear the road. If the law doesn't come soon enough, we'll bring in the bodies and leave them at the funeral home." The Stetson man tried to peek around Robert. "I trust Miss Moon is fine."

"Fit as a fiddle," Robert replied, coldly. "I'll

collect those injured men and be off. Thank you again, and chin chin." He nodded to the Pinkertons to gather their associates.

The Stetson man tipped the brim of his hat.

Robert walked back with the Pinkerton men, all the while wondering if he was going to be shot in the back. Once safely ensconced in the first car with Mona, he turned to her. "You'll never guess who turned out to be our savior."

Mona pulled her blanket over Robert. "Who?"

"Margaret Daly. She ordered the Stetson man to follow us."

"She could have ordered him to start the avalanche."

"I thought it odd myself that her man happened to arrive a short time after the avalanche. I'll guess we'll never know the real truth, but she did warn you of danger, Mona." Robert lit a cigarette as his nerves were frayed. "What do you want to do now?"

Mona didn't chide Robert about smoking as she knew he was upset. She was disturbed as well. "We've got three managers to deal with. We need to stay in Montana until this mess is cleared up."

"We got out by the skin of our teeth tonight,

Mona, and two of our men didn't make it. We need to make changes fast, and then get the heck out of here."

"I don't like putting our men and ourselves in danger, but we've got to see this through, Robert."

A Pinkerton knocked on the car window.

Mona rolled it down.

"Sorry, folks, but we need to put one of the injured men in this car. It's pretty tight in the other vehicle."

"Assuredly, bring him here," Robert said, before turning to his wife. "I'll drive and we'll put two men in the back."

Mona got out and stood aside as Pinkertons carried their injured comrade. They eased him into the back of the car. Mona took off her blanket, wrapping it around the injured man. She said to the non-injured Pinkerton, "You'll stay with him?"

"Ma'am, he can use my lap as his pillow. We'll get him to a hospital all right."

Mona replied, "We shall fly to the nearest hospital like the fastest hawk."

"Better make it a night owl."

Mona gave a ghost of a smile at the Pinkerton's jest. She slid into the front seat and turned to Robert. "We're ready. Let's get back to Butte."

Robert took off the emergency brake and depressed the clutch, putting the car in first gear. The car began to roll downward and Robert put the car in second gear. "Here we go, ready or not."

But Mona didn't hear Robert. She was deep in thought planning her next move.

Someone was going to pay for the death of those two men as well as Piotr Wojcik and Dr. Driscoll.

Someone indeed.

26

Early the next morning, Mamie Bannock gasped in surprise and embarrassment when she opened her front door to be greeted by Mona standing with Dexter and several Pinkertons. She clutched the throat of her dressing gown and ran her long fingers through her hair in an effort to tame it. "Miss Moon! I wasn't expecting you. Oh, my gosh, I must look a fright."

"I know it is rude to drop in like this unannounced, especially so early in the morning," Mona said, "but is Mr. Bannock present? We wish to speak with him."

"Yes, of course."

"May we enter?"

Blushing, Mamie pulled the front door wide and led Mona, Dexter, and two Pinkertons inside her front parlor. Before she closed the door, she noticed a car, parked in front of her house, with several more Pinkertons waiting.

"Greg! Miss Moon is here to see you!" Hearing footsteps upstairs, Mamie said, "He's coming. If you will excuse me, I'll be getting dressed." She and her husband passed each other on the staircase.

Mr. Bannock looked pale as he glanced at Mona and Dexter waiting for him. He hurriedly threw on his suit coat before greeting them. "Miss Moon. Mr. Deatherage. I hope you've come to set me free from house arrest." He gave a toothy grin.

"Let's go into the dining room and sit at the table," Dexter suggested. "We have some papers to go over."

"Yes, let's," Bannock said, rubbing his hands together.

Mona asked, "Mr. Bannock, are your children home?"

"They are in school."

"Good. Is Mrs. Bannock the only other person here?"

"Yes, Miss Moon. It's just us two. Why?"

"When Mrs. Bannock comes down, you are to instruct her to go with this gentleman here." Mona pointed to a Pinkerton who stepped forward. "He will take her to anywhere she wants to go—grocery store, run errands, get her hair fixed—all expenses paid by me."

"Why would you do that? Hey, what's this all about?" Bannock looked back and forth between Dexter and Mona.

Dexter said quietly, "Do as we instruct, Mr. Bannock. We hate to involve your wife and children with this—or alert the papers."

Mr. Bannock's shoulders fell as he lowered his head. "It will look funny for her to be seen with a strange man. People will talk."

Mona said, "Our man will act as her chauffeur for the day as we conduct business with you. That's the story she will tell if asked. He will be very discreet. There will be no gossip," Mona paused, "about your wife."

Mamie cheerfully bounded down the stairs and entered the dining room. The sight of Mona, Dexter, and her husband glumly sitting around the table with two Pinkertons positioned behind them gave Mamie a sudden fright. "Let me make some coffee."

Mr. Bannock stood. "That won't be necessary, dear. Miss Moon and Mr. Deatherage are here to conduct business, so Miss Moon has planned a day of enchantment for you." He pointed to the Pinkerton who gave a quick bow. "This man will drive you anywhere you want to go—to see your friends, have luncheon out, get your hair done—all on Miss Moon's dime. Isn't that nice of her?"

Mamie's eyes widened. "Really?"

Mona stood up from the dining chair. "Please, have fun today. Grab your coat and feel free to take a few friends to lunch. Enjoy yourself while your ball and chain discusses the future of Moon Mine with us."

"Oh, thank you. So thoughtful, Miss Moon. Let me grab my coat and purse," Mamie said, gleefully.

Mr. Bannock watched his wife leave with the Pinkerton and heard the car drive off. "Give me your word, you won't hurt Mamie."

"Miss Mamie is going to have lunch with a few friends and have a splendid day. It is more than I can say for you, Mr. Bannock."

"You are causing me great distress, Miss

Moon. You keep implying I have done something wrong. I have always worked in the best interest of Moon Mine, and I resent the implication otherwise."

Dexter snorted and glanced at Mona. "Shall we start?"

"Yes," Mona said, giving the signal for the remaining Pinkerton to leave.

"What's this all about?" Mr. Bannock complained.

Dexter pulled papers from his satchel and laid them on the table. "I have a sworn affidavit from Otto that you and he conspired to embezzle from Moon Enterprises."

Mr. Bannock leaned back in his chair and scoffed, "Everyone knows Otto is a scoundrel and a drunk. He will say anything to save his skin."

"Then explain these," Dexter said, pulling out photostats and placing them before Bannock. "These are copies of a second set of accounting books found in Otto's outhouse. They don't seem to match the official accounting books."

"That stupid fool," Bannock muttered, tugging at his neck collar. "Stupid, stupid fool of a man. I told him not to leave a paper trail."

"Then you confess?" Dexter asked.

"I will say nothing more without an attorney," Bannock spat out.

Mona said, "We want to know who else was involved."

"What's that noise?" Bannock asked, looking startled.

"That's our men searching your house for money and other evidence," Mona said. "Look, Bannock. We are here to make a deal—to make it easier on your family when you are sent to prison for the murder of Dr. Driscoll."

Bannock slammed his hands on the dining room table. "You must be out of your mind if you think I had anything to do with that. I was in the car with Montrose and Lacoste when Driscoll died. I was long gone before the doctor was dead."

Dexter asked, "How do you know what time Driscoll was murdered?"

"It was in the papers about the time Driscoll was thought to have died. The paper said he hanged himself. It was suicide. Everyone knows it."

"Do they?" Mona asked. "There is going to be an inquest, and I will present evidence showing Driscoll did not commit suicide, but that he was murdered."

Feeling cornered and fearful a murder was going to be pinned on him, Bannock begged, "I will make a deal with you. If you take care of my family, I will plead guilty to fraud and embezzlement, but I will not take the fall for Driscoll."

"What do you know about the man's death?"

"Do we have a deal?" Bannock asked, looking hopefully at Mona. "You've seen Mamie—almost childlike she is. You must promise to take care of her and my children."

Mona simply nodded and said, "Yes."

Bannock breathed a sigh of relief and spilled the beans. "Dr. Driscoll told Lacoste that he knew Wheedle did not kill Piotr Wojcik because he had treated Wheedle for a knife wound. It was at the same time of Wojcik's death, and Driscoll said he could prove Wheedle was innocent."

"How?" Dexter asked.

"Each doctor keeps a ledger where he notates the patient's name, medical issue, treatment, medicine, time, date, and payment amount.

Driscoll had no secretary, so the entries would have been written in his own handwriting."

"How did you find out about it?" Mona asked.

"Lacoste repeated the story to Montrose and myself."

Dexter asked, "What were your thoughts on Driscoll's statements?"

"I told Driscoll to keep his information to himself. Otto told me there were wild rumors about paid agents infiltrating from other mines who wanted to stop Moon miners from organizing. I thought Wojcik's death had to do with that because those union-busting boys like to play hardball. I was here during the 1920s, where killing over unions was an everyday occurrence, but Driscoll didn't listen to my advice. He went to the law and showed them the ledger. You see what happened."

"Where's the ledger now?" Mona asked, taking off her black leather gloves. She was becoming hot, and Bannock's story depressed her.

Bannock shrugged. "Your guess is as good as mine. If someone did murder Driscoll, then he has the ledger. Probably burned it by now."

Mona believed Bannock. He was a thief but no murderer. "You are making about 2500 per annum. Very few people in the States make that much money. Why did you steal from me and make the miners' lives so miserable?"

"It's very simple. I like to gamble and got in over my head playing poker with some unsavory folks. They threatened my family if I didn't pay up. I needed to pay the pot plus interest, but I was broke. I needed money fast, so I decided to try a little pilfering. It worked and I paid back what I owed these guys. The problem was once I started stealing, I couldn't stop. I approached Otto, who was willing to help as long as he got a cut. You were so far away, and the other managers were focused on their own jobs. Montrose and Lacoste never interfered. Oh, they complained about the lack of money for improvements from time to time, but I would show them invoices of how expensive it was to maintain the road and fix the plumbing, etcetera, etcetera—so they went about their business. I could make up invoices that looked convincing and with the stealing from the store, Otto and I made off like bandits."

"Was there anything wrong with the septic tanks?" Mona asked.

Bannock licked his lips before answering. "No, Otto and I sabotaged their installment, dug them back out, and sold most of them for new housing in Bitterroot Valley as well as the piping and toilets."

Mona closed her eyes and swayed for a moment.

Dexter asked, "Mona, are you all right?"

"I have worked nonstop for almost two years, striving to be a good steward to my employees, but then someone comes along and just uproots all good intentions. I don't know if there is enough fat in the budget to replace the septic tanks and rerun the waterlines. Copper prices have fallen from 29.5 cents per pound to 10.3 cents." Mona was so furious, she wanted to slap Bannock's face. Instead, she snapped, "Bannock, do you think it is fair for women and children to run out in the freezing cold to go to dirty outhouses while you have an indoor toilet in both your home and office, not to mention a working shower with hot water?"

"I know I sound like a miserable man," Bannock admitted.

Dexter asked, "Were Lacoste and Montrose involved in any scheme?"

Bannock shook his head. "They are both on the up and up. Just bad managers and stupid."

Mona asked, "Where's the money? You must have hidden it in this house because we've searched Otto's place and your office. The bank says you have no deposit box with them."

"There's two thousand dollars in the left rear hubcap on my car," Bannock said, afraid of Mona's fury. "I spent the rest of it on Mamie. I told her I got a fat bonus."

"How much did you and Otto swindle Moon Enterprises all together?" Dexter asked.

Bannock hesitated before confessing. He saw that Mona's fists were balled up. "About six thousand in total."

"There's your Mooncrest Village budget, Mona," Dexter said. "It would just about cover all that needs to be done."

Mona spat out, "Here's the deal, Bannock. I will not press charges if you sign a Non-Disclosure Agreement, turn over the deed to your house and other properties, and make restitution for the total amount to the last penny including a thousand dollar personal loan from me to start over in some other town. But you are to leave Montana immediately with your family and only return if you are needed to testify. My men will be watching you constantly, so there is no escape. If I press charges, Mamie will divorce you. You will be left without a family, a job, standing in any community, and you will go to prison. Your wife, children, neighbors will shun you."

"I will do anything you want but please don't disgrace me. I love my wife. I don't want her hurt. Please. Please for her sake. I'll do anything you want. Just have mercy, Miss Moon," Bannock pleaded as tears ran down his face.

Satisfied she had broken Bannock, Mona pushed away from the dining table, leaving Dexter to deal with the scoundrel. She had solved the Mooncrest Village debacle, but she still had not solved the Driscoll and Wojcik murders, but she was getting closer.

It was only a matter of time before Mona learned the truth.

27

Returning to Mooncrest Village the next day, Rupert stoked up the fire in the potbellied stove. "It will be warm in a minute."

Mona sat behind Dr. Driscoll's desk. "Rupert, Moon Mine is falling apart. I have no manager for Mooncrest Village, no doctor for the miners, and no employee for the store."

"Yes, but you've rooted out the corruption. A wound hurts the most before it starts healing."

Mona held up a finger. "I've rooted out part of the corruption."

"You still think Bannock had nothing to do with Driscoll's murder?"

"He's a thief, but he's no murderer. He's too much of a powder-puff."

"You think?"

Mona shrugged. "I think. Sometimes all one has to go on is a gut feeling. I feel Bannock had nothing to do with Driscoll's death."

Rupert asked, "Can you tell me why we are in this ice cube stand?"

"I got a crazy thought last night." Mona leaned her elbows on the desk. "Driscoll knew the ledger was important. Maybe he hid it."

Rupert replied, "It is more likely it was taken by his murderers."

Mona continued, "Let's just pretend Driscoll hid the ledger and had planned on taking it with him, but his murderers attacked before the doctor could get to it. They couldn't find it as they didn't have much time."

"Okay, let's say it's a possibility. They couldn't come back to search since the house was under watch by your men. I can see that if Driscoll hid the ledger—and that is 'if.'"

Mona surveyed the doctor's office. "Where would you have hidden the ledger, Rupert?"

"Driscoll would need quick access. Let's look under his desk."

Mona pulled out drawers and looked at their bottoms while Rupert crawled under the wooden desk.

Both were disappointed when they found nothing.

Rupert snapped his fingers. "I have an idea. What if Driscoll was not assaulted in the building? We found nothing broken, nothing that indicated a struggle—just that his suitcase had been unpacked. What if Driscoll was jumped outside as he was going to collect the ledger?"

"It would have to be somewhere dry or else the ink would fade."

Both Mona and Rupert rushed outside and stood scanning the property. There were no outbuildings, wells, or forked trees where something could be hidden.

"Perhaps he gave the ledger to someone?" Rupert suggested.

Mona shook her head. "Driscoll was too afraid to bring someone else into this. He didn't trust anyone after the sheriff scoffed at him."

"Well, I'm at a loss, Mona. I don't know where to look."

"What about the gutters?"

Rupert answered, "He wouldn't have been able to keep the ledger dry and there is no ladder."

Mona spotted one lonely rain barrel near a spout. "Hey, Rupert, look at this."

Rupert replied sarcastically, "Yeah, it's a rain barrel, Mona."

Mona peered into the barrel. "You have a rain barrel just like this, but yours is frozen solid with ice. This barrel is empty."

"Let me look." Rupert pushed Mona aside and tipped the barrel over. "You're right. This barrel should be filled with frozen water."

They both studied the ground wondering if the ledger had been buried.

"The ground is too hard to dig. This is another dead end," Rupert said. "I'm getting cold. Let's go back inside."

"You big baby," Mona shot back. She tapped the clapboards on the house that were situated behind the now removed barrel. "Rupert, this board feels loose."

Reluctantly, Rupert got out a pen knife and thrust the blade behind the loose board, wiggling it free. Rupert squatted down and peered into the hole left by the removed board. "There's something in here, Mona." He pulled at another board and then another until he and Mona were staring at a yellow, oilskin raincoat. Rupert pulled the raincoat out and unwrapped it.

There lay what Dr. Driscoll had been killed for—his medical ledger in pristine condition!

28

Days later on a Saturday morning, Mona knocked on Tessie's door.

Tessie opened the door dusting flour from her hands. "Oh, good Lord! Miss Mona. Come in. Come in."

"I said I would come to see you before I left. I also wanted you to meet my companion, Violet, and this is my dog, Chloe."

"How do you do?" Tessie said, extending her hand until she saw flour on it, giving a quick laugh. "You must excuse me. This is baking day."

"It smells divine in here," Violet commented, as Chloe pulled on her leash.

"I'm frying up some donuts."

Violet said, "We've met before—at the tea."

"I'm so sorry for not recognizing you. That

day was such a whirlwind with the tea and then Dr. Driscoll's death."

"Yes, it was an extreme day for everyone," Mona said, noticing a man standing with a newspaper in his hand. He was quite large with black bushy eyebrows and raven hair in need of a haircut.

Tessie rushed over and placed a hand on the man's burly chest. "This is my husband, Johnny."

Both Mona and Violet nodded hello.

Johnny waved his free hand. "Please sit." He seemed confused about the purpose of Mona's visit. The couple was not accustomed to entertaining guests in their humble shack, especially the famous owner of Moon Mine.

Mona and Violet politely sat while Tessie scrambled to pour coffee and place warm donuts on plates.

Mona said, "Tessie, please sit down. I want to talk to you and your husband."

"Me? You want to talk to me, ma'am?" Johnny asked, surprised.

"Yes, please sit with us. I have something to ask."

Tessie and Johnny quickly sat down and folded their hands on top of the table. They glanced at each other before turning their attention to Mona and Violet.

"Tessie, you told me that you knew basic bookkeeping, typing, filing, and purchasing of goods."

"That's right. I worked at a church."

"I remembered. I contacted the church you work for, and they gave a glowing recommendation. Said they were sorry to lose you."

Tessie smiled. "That's nice to hear. Isn't it, Johnny?"

Johnny nodded.

They both became silent again and stared at Mona and Violet.

Mona cleared her throat before speaking. "As you know the village store has been closed since Otto left. We need someone with bookkeeping and management skills. The village also needs someone to keep the road maintained, mow, collect garbage, and keep the village clean. I want to know if you two would be interested in managing Mooncrest Village and the store."

Flabbergasted, Tessie grabbed her husband's hand and spoke, "I don't know if I have the know-how to do so. I worked for a poor, country church."

"The principles are the same. Rupert Hunt will be staying on to help with the transition. He knows how I want things run since we are instituting new protocols."

Tessie glanced at her husband. "I don't know. Should I, honey?"

"It's up to you, Tessie girl," Johnny replied. "You do what you think is right."

"What about Johnny?" Tessie asked.

Mona explained, "I've asked around about you, sir, as well. You are acquainted with heavy machinery and since you are from a farming background, you know how to work outdoors. We need a man to help Tessie with the heavy lifting like I said—mowing, grading the road— that sort of thing. You will be provided with housing and each paid eight hundred dollars per annum with a bonus at Christmas if the Village and store are in tip-top condition. There will be inspections throughout the year."

Tessie's eyes widened. "Eight hundred each?"

"Yes. Each," Mona replied.

Tessie appeared stunned.

"That's lower than what I'm paid working in the mine," Johnny said.

Mona reiterated, "Yes, but there is the free housing, use of a car plus any Moon Mine truck, gas, twenty-percent employee discount at the store, a Christmas bonus plus no threat of a mining accident. Tessie would not have to bake to make ends meet unless she wants to. You and Tessie would be in a better financial situation than most people."

"We will take it," Johnny said, putting his arm around Tessie. "I hate to tell you this, Miss Moon, but I don't like mining much. It's a filthy, dangerous profession."

Tessie said quickly, "Please don't be insulted, Mona. Johnny talks too much."

Mona replied, "I'm not insulted, Miss Tessie. Mining is a hard way to make a living."

"We'll shake hands and the deal is done," Johnny said, extending his calloused hand.

"Yes, we will shake on it," Mona said, grinning. She shook Tessie's and Johnny's hands. "Dexter Deatherage will be here this afternoon with a contract. Get some rest because Rupert Hunt will be here bright and early Monday morning to help you both settle in and turn over the keys. The store is to open at nine sharp."

"We will be ready. We will meet Rupert at the store," Johnny said.

"Good. Good." Mona and Violet rose to leave.

"Wait! You must take some donuts with you," Tessie said, rushing to fill a brown paper bag.

"We will take them gladly," Violet said, almost licking her lips. She realized she was hungry.

Chloe jumped up on a chair to get closer to a donut on a plate.

"Get down, Chloe," Violet ordered.

Ignoring the poodle, Johnny raised his newspaper. "I must ask something before you leave, Miss Moon. I bummed a ride into town to get this newspaper." He held the front page up displaying a large black banner headline—WHEEDLE HAS ALIBI! ALL CHARGES DROPPED!

"Is the mischief over, Miss Mona?" Tessie asked.

Mona replied, "Rupert and I found Dr. Driscoll's medical ledger which proved Wheedle's whereabouts during Wojcik's murder. I'm glad we could free Wheedle."

Tessie fretted, "No matter the proof, people will still believe Wheedle killed Wojcik."

"People can think what they want, but they should leave the man alone."

"I hear Wheedle's going back to the reservation," Johnny announced, glancing at his wife for confirmation.

Violet said, "Do you blame him for wanting to get away from white men?"

Johnny shook his head. "No, miss, I don't, but if Wheedle didn't kill Wojcik, who did?"

Mona said, "We might never know, and that's the unfortunate truth of the matter."

As Mona and Violet started for the door, Mona turned, "I forgot something. I met one of Dr. Driscoll's patients—a Karl Steiner? I haven't seen him since."

Johnny made a sour face. "That putz."

Tessie admonished, "No, Johnny. No bad talk on such a happy day."

Mona insisted, "Let him speak, Tessie. I want to hear what Johnny has to say."

Johnny folded the newspaper. "Steiner is a galoot, always bellyaching about this and that, spouting off about books he had read saying the working man is being abused. Now I couldn't argue with the man's thinking, but he wouldn't let it lie there. Said we had to rise up and kill our taskmasters. I asked him once—if we kill our bosses, who is going to pay us? He said we'd rob banks. Steiner talked bunk all the time and was worthless on the job. I hated working a shift with him. Steiner would disappear down shafts not assigned and barely met his quota. I never trusted the man. Thought he bordered on being one of those anarchists."

"What was Steiner's explanation for leaving his crew?" Mona asked.

Johnny shifted his weight. "Said he heard noises and wanted to investigate. Total bull. Please excuse my language."

"Do you know where he might be now?"

"I haven't seen Steiner for days. He hasn't shown up for work. Not since Driscoll hanged himself."

Mona didn't correct Johnny on the cause of Driscoll's death. The truth would come out in the inquest held on Monday. "Is the cast off his leg now?"

Johnny sneered. "That's another thing. He

had only a hairline fracture on his ankle bone. Montrose put him on light duty where he could sit, but Steiner insisted on a big plaster cast and bed rest—the whole works. The rest of us are digging out copper with cuts, abrasions, and torn ligaments, but he can't even work sitting from a chair in the supervisor's office. Like I said, Steiner was a putz."

"Did he have any friends?"

"Yeah, two guys who held similar beliefs. They lived together in number forty-nine. Always reading books in German."

"And the three of them are gone?"

"All three of them. Look, I'm all for improving things for the working man, but I stop at hurting people. There was too much violence in the 1920's."

"Thank you, Johnny, for being so frank. I appreciate it."

"Why are you interested in Karl Steiner?" Johnny asked.

"Did I say I was interested?" Mona gave Tessie and Johnny a wide grin before she and Violet stepped out into the brisk air. "Let's go back to the hotel, Violet."

Violet asked, "Are you interested in this Karl Steiner?"

"I am looking for discontented men who have very little impulse control with Napoleon-like egos."

Violet teased, "That describes half the men I know."

Mona picked up Chloe so the dog wouldn't get her paws dirty in the slushy snow. "I may be reaching at straws, but Steiner fits the classic profile of a saboteur. He sounds very much like a tomb raider I knew in Mesopotamia, but that man's goal was money, not ideology."

Violet, who had been reading about the miners' fights with the mine owners in Butte, said, "It also fits the typical Pinkerton man. They busted many a head breaking up strikes."

"All those killers had to do was retrieve the medical ledger to destroy evidence, but they killed Driscoll out of spite." Mona held out her arms so Chloe could jump in the back seat. "Let's not discuss it here. People are staring out their windows. Let's wave to everyone."

Mona and Violet turned in each direction and waved. Many a curtain flung closed, but some of the women came out of their stoops, signaling goodbye with handkerchiefs or scarves. Mona and Violet got inside their chauffeur driven Packard and rolled down the windows, waving until they drove out of Mooncrest Village. Even Chloe stuck her head out the back window and barked.

Monday was the inquest day, and everyone would learn Dr. Driscoll was murdered. After the inquest, Mona, Robert, and the rest of her team were scheduled to take the evening train. Although Mona hated the thought of ditching Butte without discovering the identity of Wojcik's and Driscoll's murderers, it was time for her and Robert to move on.

She would leave Rupert Hunt behind to continue digging for the truth. It was the only thing she could do.

29

Three hours after Mona and Violet had visited Tessie, Rupert arrived at Mona's hotel suite, overcoat dirty and his hat covered in fine dust. "Sorry about this, but I came straight from the mine," he said, looking down at his filthy clothes.

Violet helped Rupert off with his coat and took his hat. "I'm going to shake off some of the grime," she said before leaving. She knew Mona wanted to hear Rupert's report alone.

"What did you find out?" Mona asked, pouring the man a cup of hot coffee.

Rupert took the cup gratefully and sipped. "Are these Tessie's donuts?"

Mona handed him the donut plate. He took two and was stuffing one in his mouth when Robert walked in, throwing his hat and coat on a chair. "Hello, Rupert."

"Lord Bob," Rupert greeted him."

Robert said to Mona, "The Pinkerton lads are doing well and should be discharged from the hospital before we leave on Monday."

"That's good to hear."

"I told them about their comrades not making it. They were glum, but they took the news on the chin. However, neither one can remember a thing. Doctor said that was normal after an accident, but their memory might recover—*might* being the operative word."

"Thank you for going to the hospital, Robert," Mona said, grasping his hand as he sat next to her. They both looked expectantly at Rupert.

Rupert swallowed and took another sip of coffee before giving his report. "It was as you suspected, Mona. I checked Steiner's cabin and he and his roommates have cleared out. Clothes, suitcases, personal items—all gone, but I found this." He reached into his pocket, retrieving several crumpled, half-burnt letters and handed them to Mona.

Mona read the letters quickly. "This is very disturbing. The letters are urging Steiner to use violence."

"Look at the signature, Mona."

Mona skimmed the bottom of one of the letters and gasped. "Emma Goldman!"

"The anarchist?" Robert sputtered, grabbing one of the letters from Mona's hands. "Has this signature been verified?"

"We're working on verifying Goldman's handwriting," Rupert replied. "That's not all. We found all sorts of radical political pamphlets strewn about Steiner's cabin. Once the handwriting is verified, we will be able to connect Steiner as a Goldman disciple and fellow anarchist."

"Do you think he and his buddies worked in concert with one of the competing mining companies?"

"I think these birds worked alone. They are idealogues. This is not about money for them."

Mona asked, "What about the mine? Johnny said Steiner would disappear down unmanned tunnels."

"You were right to be suspicious after listening to Johnny. The demolition team discovered two bombs in shafts that were not being used, but would have caused other producing tunnels to collapse."

Mona raised an eyebrow. "I wonder why the bombs were not set off."

"I think they were set to explode on the day of your official arrival at Mooncrest Village, but Steiner somehow discovered Driscoll was leaving with you and had to choose between blowing up the mine or getting rid of him."

"But why?" Robert asked.

Mona explained, "I think I know. It must have been Steiner or one of his buddies who killed Wojcik, afraid Driscoll's evidence would set Wheedle free. They wanted Wheedle to take the fall for Wojcik. That's why Steiner insisted on a plaster cast and bed rest at the medical office, so he could keep an eye on Driscoll. Someone from the sheriff's office must have blabbed about Driscoll's insisting that Wheedle was innocent."

"And word got back to Steiner. He self-inflicted trauma, causing a slight fracture. He used his time in the infirmary looking for the ledger, but couldn't locate it," Robert said, coming to the obvious conclusion.

Mona thought out loud. "One of the three must have seen me with Driscoll at his office and decided the doctor knew too much and was going to turn the ledger over. Poor Dr. Driscoll—in the wrong place at the wrong time." She took a sip of coffee, hoping the hot drink would soothe her nerves. "Where do we go from here?"

Rupert said, "I gave an order for the Pinkertons and my network to search for Steiner and his friends in three states. They are searching bus stops, trains, hotels—you name it—if it has wheels they are checking it out, but I think our rats have probably split up. This search is going to cost you a pretty penny, Mona."

"After the inquest on Monday, the police will hopefully take over. Robert and I will testify, and Dexter will present our evidence. That should be enough to spur the authorities forward. I will also send a personal telegram to the governor asking him to assist with the hunt."

"That should do it then." Rupert looked at his wristwatch and jumped up, calling for Violet. "You got my threads, sweets."

Violet emerged from the bathroom with Rupert's things. "Here you go. Clean as a whistle, but you should see the dirty tub. I brushed your things off in it."

Rupert grabbed his hat and coat, winking at

Violet. "You and I should step out sometime."

"In your dreams, Rupert."

He grinned and shoved his hat on. "You can't blame a man from trying, honey bun."

Violet rolled her eyes.

Mona and Robert followed Rupert to the elevator.

He doffed his hat to Mona, "I'll set Tessie up on Monday morning and hightail it to the inquest. Until then."

Mona nodded as her stomach lurched. Everything rode on the inquest's findings. She wondered if justice would be served.

30

It was nine-thirty when Mona, Robert, and Dexter arrived at the courthouse for the inquest. Dexter hung back while Mona and Robert stood on the steps allowing the photographers to take their pictures. After a minute, Robert waved them off and escorted Mona inside. Finding the chamber where the inquest was being held, they took seats in front where other witnesses sat.

"ALL STAND" a clerk commanded, as the black-robed judge strode in and took his seat behind the bench. A jury had been empanelled, and the judge swore them in to open the proceedings.

The sheriff testified first, giving his spin on Dr. Gene Driscoll's death. Then the county coroner testified, proclaiming Driscoll's death was a suicide.

Mona was called to testify, and she related her conversation with Dr. Driscoll on the day of his death. Since the inquest was informally conducted, the judge asked Mona questions. Did she believe Dr. Driscoll's death was a suicide?

"I most certainly do not. His death was a murder, and I have proof to back that statement, if the Court will allow introduction of the evidence."

The courtroom lit up with buzzing from the reporters and spectators.

The judge called for quiet in the courtroom before continuing his questioning of Mona. "Do you have anything to add, Mrs. Farley?"

"Only that the Court allow Mr. Deatherage to present evidence contrary to the judgment of suicide."

The judge looked at Dexter Deatherage. "Sir, do you have a license to practice law in the state of Montana?"

"No, your honor, but Moon Enterprises has hired a Montana lawyer to officially present evidence with me assisting, if it pleases the Court."

"Do you have any witnesses, Mr. Deatherage?"

"I do, your honor."

"So be it," the judge said. "Mrs. Farley, please step down. Those presenting evidence, stand. Let's do this once and save time. Raise your right hand to be sworn in."

Dexter and his Montana law associate stood, as well as a calligraphy expert, the Montana state medical examiner, a fingerprint expert, the Pinkerton who took photographs of the crime scene, and men from the Moon Mine, who would testify about the bombs and radical statements made by Karl Steiner.

After two hours of testimony, the jury was excused for deliberations.

Hungry and spent, Mona, Robert, Dexter were leaving the courthouse, when they stopped again to pose for photographers on the portico.

The reporters shouted at Mona. "Miss Moon, turn this way! Give us a smile! What's it like being a duchess now? Do you think the jury will find in your favor? What was your relationship with Dr. Driscoll?"

Over the reporters, Mona heard a shout, "MONA! LOOK OUT! HE'S GOT A GUN!"

Robert threw Mona aside shielding her with

his back exposed to the threat.

A shot sounded, silence, and then screams.

Deputies pushed past Robert and Mona, running down the courthouse steps.

"Are you all right, dear?" Robert asked, huskily.

"Yes, are you?"

"Yes." He turned to Dexter, who was staring at the crowd. "Dexter?"

Dexter said candidly, "I think I need a change of trousers."

"Righto," Robert replied. "Me, too. What happened?"

Dexter said, "Karl Steiner pushed his way through the crowd and pointed a gun at us."

"Did he get the shot off?"

"No, Steiner was killed."

"Who shouted the warning?"

"The man who killed Steiner." Dexter pointed to the crowd where Rupert Hunt stood with a gun in his hand. A deputy took it from him.

Robert and Rupert's eyes met. Robert gave him a nod of thanks before he whisked Mona back into the courthouse where they left by a basement entryway.

An hour later at the hotel, they received word the jury had delivered a judgment of homicide for Dr. Driscoll's death.

31

Mona was depressed as she knew the sheriff would find a way to determine Steiner was a lone wolf and would never search for Steiner's two conspirators. He would blame Steiner for Wojcik's and Driscoll's murders, the bombs, and the avalanche deaths.

Mona would never know if Steiner acted solely out of political conviction or if he had been spurred by her mining competitors. She would just have to live with the uncertainty. Mona pulled Robert close to her. "Robert, it's time to leave and put this behind us. Rupert and Dexter can handle things from here."

"I agree, my American cow. The honeymoon shall go forth as planned."

"And to think we went almost two weeks

without you referring to me as a cow."

Robert responded by giving Mona a passionate kiss. When he came up for air, Robert said, "The honeymoon starts now!"

"Thank goodness," Mona replied, shutting their bedroom door with her foot.

Violet had been passing through the parlor when she heard the lock on Mona's bedroom snap shut. Grinning, she said to Chloe, "I think you and I will hurry to my bedroom down the hall. Those two have lost time to make up, and I think they'll appreciate us being out of earshot."

It turned out Mona and Robert missed the evening train, and no one saw them for the next two days. When they emerged from their cocoon, Mona glowed and Robert seemed very pleased with himself.

Hand in hand, they left the hotel, ready to face the future together, knowing another adventure was sure to await them.

The above is the alchemy symbol for copper.

1934 Indian Reorganization Act (IRA)

On June 18, 1934, President Roosevelt signs into law the Wheedle-Howard Act, recognizing the right of self-determination for Native Americans instead of assimilation into European-American culture. The law restored ownership of millions of tribal lands plus mineral rights, provided 4.4 million in loans for livestock and farm equipment, and restored freedom of religious and tribal customs. As the tribes were to vote on acceptance of the IRA, they split their votes between traditional versus progressive votes creating schisms within the tribes. Overall, the progressive Native American vote won. A total of 266 tribes voted to accept the IRA, while 77 rejected it. There have been attempts by Congressional members and local/state agencies to dismantle the IRA throughout the years. So far, their attempts have proven unsuccessful.

Apparently, the 1934 IRA Act was not enough. In 1975, Congress passed the Indian

Self-Determination and Education Assistance Act allowing Native peoples to operate their own schools and work with the U. S. Government for federal services. This law was enacted after the 1950s and 1960s Termination Policy where Native Americans were encouraged to leave the reservations and move to urban areas. The goal of the Termination Policy was to dismantle reservations.

Absaroka

Unhappy with the dispersal of federal funds to urban area, ranchers and farmers proposed to create a new state called Absaroka out of southern Montana, northern Wyoming, and western part of South Dakota. Bubbling since 1934, the movement became official in 1935 and forced administrators to look at redistribution of federal aid to rural areas. A. R. Swickard, a street commissioner, declared himself governor of Absaroka. The movement died out completely by WWII as officials parceled out more federal aid to rural areas of the three states. As a nod to this movement, Craig Johnson, author of the Walt Longmire Mysteries, has the setting of his western mysteries take place in Absaroka County.

This very same scenario was played out by parts of Oregon, which wanted to secede to Idaho in 2023.

Alice Speed Stoll (1908–1996)

As with the Charles and Anne Lindberg baby kidnapping of 1932, Mrs. Stoll's kidnapping became a national sensation. On Oct. 10, 1934, Alice Stoll, wife of a Louisville oil executive, was kidnapped from her home and taken to Indianapolis where she was beaten and kept in a darkened room. Alice Stoll was considered an *aristocrat* and *old money*. She was the niece of a former ambassador to Germany and her grandfather was Breckenridge Speed, a prominent businessman and philanthropist. The maiden name of Miss Alice adorns the *Speed Art Museum* in Louisville, so you get the picture. Her husband, Berry Stoll's wealth came from oil refineries and gas stations across Kentucky.

Her kidnapper was Thomas Robinson, a one-time law student at Vanderbilt University who went from being an inmate at a Tennessee insane asylum to the FBI's top 10 most wanted list. The ransom was paid, Mrs. Stoll was freed, and Robinson was captured years later disguised as a woman. Robinson was tried and given the death penalty, but President Truman commuted the sentence. Mrs. Stoll passed away in 1996, leaving a 156 million dollar estate.

Anaconda Mine (1881–1982)

Marcus Daly bought the Anaconda Silver Mine in Butte, Montana and discovered copper. Daly decided to concentrate on the copper instead of silver. Daly knew copper would be in demand and the price would skyrocket, because Thomas Edison had developed the light bulb. As an immigrant Irishman, he recruited immigrants from Ireland. They flocked to the Anaconda Mine as Daly kept his promises of training and good pay. Daly sold majority interest the Anaconda Mine to the Rockefellers in 1899 with Standard Oil as the umbrella company. Daly died in 1900.

Because shaft mining was so expensive, the Anaconda Mine switched to open pit mining in 1947—the Berkeley Pit, which is a tourist attraction and environmental disaster. All operations for the Anaconda Mine in Butte were shut down in 1982 on Earth Day. From 1892 to 1903, the Anaconda Mine was the largest producing copper mine in the world. It produced $300 billion worth of metal such as copper, aluminum, gold, uranium, zinc, and silver.

Anaconda Mine Road Massacre (April 21st, 1920)

The Industrial Workers of the World (Wobblies) and the Metal Mine Workers Industrial Union called for a strike of all mines surrounding Butte, Montana. The workers wanted better pay, eight-hour work day, and an end to worker harassment due to unionizing. Anaconda Copper Mining Company fired upon picketing miners, killing a Tom Manning and shooting sixteen fleeing miners in the back. Tom Manning's killer was never brought to justice. The massacre was the last major conflict in Butte until the 1934 National Recovery Act, allowing outside support to help rebuild the Butte Miner's Union. A good book to read is Dashiell Hammett's *Red Harvest*. He was a Pinkerton, trained in union busting, before he started writing mystery stories like *The Thin Man* and *The Maltese Falcon*.

Likewise, three years before the strike, an IWW organizer, Frank Little, was beaten and hanged from a railroad trestle. His murderers were never tried.

Anarchists
People who believe in personal autonomy and the dismantling of government and religious hierarchies.

Bank Closings (1932–)
In 1932, banks closed their doors when they did not have enough cash on hand to give to their depositors. The panic caused a run on banks and 1400 banks closed. They lost 725 million in total deposits. In 1933, having been sworn in as president only thirty-six hours earlier, President Roosevelt issued Proclamation 2039 on 1 a.m. on Monday, March 6, ordering a suspension on banking transactions for a week. The goal was to give surviving banks time to do inventory and reset. Congress, acting in concert with President Roosevelt, passed the Emergency Banking Act of 1933 on March 9 thus creating the FDIC, which guaranteed depositors' bank accounts up to $5000. Reassured, the public redeposited up to a billion dollars within the month. However, many people still put cash in a tin can and buried the can in the yard. I know this because my mother was one of many who did not trust banks. We still see banks closing today.

Bureau of Indian Affairs BIA (1775–)

The BIA was founded by U. S. Congress in 1775 as the Committee on Indian Affairs and headed by Benjamin Franklin. It oversaw trade and treaty agreements with tribes until it morphed into the Bureau of Indian Affairs in 1824 by Secretary of War, John C. Calhoun. In 1849, BIA was transferred to the Department of the Interior. The BIA has a shaded past of forced assimilation policies and corruption within its ranks. It currently provides services to 574 tribes and two million Native Americans.

British Table Manners vs American Table Manners

The British eat with a fork held by their non-dominant hand while holding a knife in their dominant hand. The knife is used to push food onto the fork. The user does not put the silverware down except to drink.

Americans hold the knife in their dominant hand to cut food and then place the knife down by the side of the plate or to a corner on the plate. The American then uses his/her dominant hand to use a fork or spoon to eat. The hand, not in use, lies in their lap. In order to drink, silverware is placed on the plate or placemat—never directly on the tablecloth. Both cultures use napkins and forbid elbows on the table unless in casual company. It is considered rude to look at your watch or place a phone on the table during a meal—even today.

Cup of Joe

The theory is that Joe is a common form of the word Jamoke which was a nickname for coffee in the 19th century. The words of Java and mocha were combined for the expression *cup of jamoke* which was shortened to a *cup of Joe.* I think this theory is a cup of nonsense but who knows. The phrase *cup of Joe* appears in writing in 1930.

I personally like the story that Josephus Daniels, the Secretary of the Navy, banned alcohol on U. S. Navy ships in 1914. Sailors then called coffee, the next strongest stimulant, a *cup of Josephus* and then shortened it to *cup of Joe.* Take your pick of tall tales.

Cut A Rug

Slang term for dancing. Term faded out in the 1940s and then reemerged briefly in the 1990s.

Daniel Boone (1734–1820)

Boone was a famous frontiersman, hunter, and explorer, who blazed the Wilderness Road through the Cumberland Gap into Kentucky which was part of Virginia at that time. The Wilderness Road was based on a Native American warrior and trading footpath through the Appalachian Mountains. He established Fort Boonesborough, which was one of the first English-speaking settlements in Kentucky. By the 1800's, more than 20,000 people had entered Kentucky via the Wilderness Road. Boone is known for inscribing *D. Boone Kilt A Bar, 1803* on a Beech tree with his knife. People during Mona Moon's time would have been very familiar with this incident and would have quoted it in a humorous fashion.

Dutch Oven

A cast iron Dutch oven was a large pot with a lid that was cooked over heat or in a fire. Mostly used for stews and soups, but one could also bake in it as well.

Dust Bowl (1932–1936, 1939–1940)

The Dust Bowl occurred in the Great Plains of

the United States when the topsoil dried out and blew away causing gigantic dust clouds. This phenomenon was caused by drought and poor agricultural practices. Illnesses such as "dust pneumonia" result when humans and animals breathe in large quantities of dust, thus inflaming the alveoli and preventing the lungs from clearing. Symptoms include difficulty in breathing, chest pain, fever, and coughing. The Red Cross made and distributed dust masks during the Dust Bowl, but it is estimated 7000 people still died. Approximately, 3.5 million people migrated from the Midwest to other states where they could have a fresh start. These people were referred to as *Okies*. Read John Steinbeck's *Grapes of Wrath*.

Blackfoot Native American

"Blackfoot" is the English translation of the word *siksika*, which means "black foot." It refers to the dark colored moccasins the indigenous people wore. Some Blackfoot people are annoyed by the plural "Blackfeet," but many Blackfoot people accept both terms.

Eleanor Roosevelt (1884–1962)

Roosevelt served as First Lady of the United

States from 1933 to 1945. During this time, Mrs. Roosevelt worked to expand the rights of working women, WWII refugees, and the civil rights of minorities. She advocated the U.S. join the United Nations and was appointed as its first delegate. Serving as first chair on the UN Commission on Human Rights, she oversaw the drafting of the Universal Declaration of Human Rights. Roosevelt later chaired President John Kennedy's Presidential Commission on the Status of Women. She was the niece of President Theodore Roosevelt and first cousin to Alice Roosevelt Longworth. Roosevelt married her fifth cousin once removed, Franklin Delano Roosevelt, who became the 32nd President of the U.S. She is considered one of the most admired people of the twentieth century.

Emma Goldman (1869–1940)

Goldman was a Russian immigrant to the United States and was well-known for her violent anarchist views. She was also a lecturer, political writer, and theorist. In 1892, she and her lover, Alexander Berkman, tried to assassinate industrialist Henry Frick, hoping to inspire workers to revolt against the capitalist system, but Frick survived the assassination attempt. Berkman was sentenced to 22 years in prison. Goldman was not arrested as the police could not tie her to the crime. She was later arrested on the charge of "inciting to riot." After the Great War, Goldman was castigated by the Communist Party for her disdain for the Marxist revolution in Russia, her birth county.

In 1901, a Leon Czolgosy killed US President William McKinley after he claimed he was inspired by a speech from Emma Goldman.

In 1933, Goldman lectured in the United States and that's when fictitious Karl Steiner would have fallen under her spell.

Dickens To Pay
An idiom—to force someone to act.

Five and Dime Stores (1879–1990)
Small local shops with a lunch counter that copied the larger department stores with a smaller selection of inexpensive goods including sewing supplies, small housewares, shoes, stationery, hosiery, candy, toiletries—items that women could carry home on their own. Woolworth is an example of a dime store and was the center of the

Civil Rights Movement with minorities demanding a right to being served at the lunch counter during the 1960s.

Friedrich Nietzsche (1844–1900)

Nietzsche was a controversial German philologist and philosopher who was the youngest person to hold the Chair of Classical Philology at the University of Basel when only 24 years of age. He quit philology and turned to philosophy. His writings would later have a profound influence on the Nazi Party, especially his concept of *Übermensch* (Superman) from his 1883 book, *Thus Spoke Zarathustra*. Zarathustra argues a shift from Christian values since "God is dead" to that of the Superman, who should be the creator of new values. The Übermensch rejects community standards of good and evil since it favors mediocrity and creates his own morality, thus becoming the Superman. During WWI, German soldiers received copies of *Thus Spoke Zarathustra* as gifts.

Nietzsche became mentally ill in 1889 and remained in his family's care until his death in 1900 from a series of strokes. His breakdown has been blamed on dementia possibly caused by anything from syphilis to manic depression with periodic psychosis. His work remains widely popular.

Great Depression (1929–1939)

The Great Depression was a world-wide phenomenon caused by the U.S. stock market crash in October 1929. The years 1931–1934 were the worst years of the Depression with an unemployment percentage rate of 15.9, 23.6, 24.9, 21.7 respectively, and even in 1940 unemployment was fifteen percent. President FDR's New Deal programs such as the CCC and the WPA helped, but it wasn't until WWII that the country roared out of the Great Depression for good.

Great War (1914–1918)

First European world war was called the Great War until WWII. Then it was called WWI.

Horace Greeley (1811–1872)

Greeley was the founder and editor of the *New-York Tribune*, which became the highest circulated paper in the country. He espoused progressive policies such as feminism, temperance, and freeing of enslaved peoples. He popularized the slogan "Go west, young man," as a solution to expand the United States boundaries and create opportunity for the unemployed.

IWW (1905–)

The Industrial Workers of the World was a labor union founded in Chicago which tried to unify all workers, regardless of race, color, skill, and gender into one giant union. Its members were called Wobblies. They used violence, strikes, and sabotage to effect change. They are still active with strikes, but now work within the law. In the 21st century, they have focused their attention on organizing workers at Starbucks, Jimmy Johns, and Whole Foods Market.

Indian

Indian was a term used by non-Indians to describe a Native American. The term *indios* was used by Christopher Columbus as he thought he had discovered India. North American indigenous people prefer to be called Native American or First Nations. Mona would still refer to First Nations people as Indians in 1934 and not see any disrespect in it, but may have by 1960 when Native American activism was strong.

Jean Harlow (1911–1937)

Harlow was an American comedic actress and one of the first sex symbols of the "talkies." Known as the "Platinum Bombshell", she became one of Hollywood's biggest stars and is still ranked at No. 22 on AFI's greatest female stars of the Golden Age of Hollywood. Those closest to Harlow called her *Baby*. Harlow died of kidney failure at the age of twenty-six.

Margaret Daly (1853–1941)

Miss Margaret was the wife of copper magnet Marcus Daly. She literally tumbled into Daly's arms when she tripped while touring a mine. They fell in love and it continued to be a love match until Marcus died in 1900. In her husband's honor, Margaret gave funds to build a hospital in Hamilton, Montana and provided an endowment for it. She gave money to the Boy Scouts of American, which allowed them to build the first scout camp in the Skalkaho area, and donated land for a library. She was fond of pearls and her jewelry was valued at $54,000 upon her death. After her husband, Marcus, died, she hired others to look after her interest in the Anaconda Mine. She passed away at Riverside, her Montana mansion.

Mesopotamia

Name for the historical region between the Tigris-Euphrates river system. Also called the Fertile Crescent. Name covers the modern countries of Kuwait, Iraq, Iran, Syria, and Turkey. The area is now referred to as the Middle East which also includes Egypt, Sudan, Saudi Arabia, and other countries.

Morpheus

Greek god associated with sleep.

New Deal

New Deal was a term taken from Franklin D. Roosevelt's acceptance speech for the presidential Democratic nomination on July 2nd, 1932. He was voted into the US presidency in November after the public reacted negatively to the ineffectiveness of President Herbert Hoover in regard to the Great Depression, which he said would only last a few weeks in 1929. By 1932, the country was dissatisfied with Hoover's policies, and Americans swept the Democratic Party into office with the promise of a "new deal" for the "forgotten man."

New Deal policies were enacted within the

first three months of Roosevelt's presidency, which became known as the "Hundred Days." Agencies such as the Works Progress Administration (WPA) and the Civilian Conservation Corps (CCC) were established to provide temporary employment. The WPA provided 8.5 million jobs, produced 650,000 miles of roads, built 125,000 public buildings, 75,000 bridges, and 8,000 parks. Also included in the national bills were the Federal Art Project, Federal Writers' Project, and the Federal Theatre Project to document the Great Depression.

Paul Bunyan

Paul Bunyan is a mythological giant lumberjack with superhuman strength in American and Canadian folklore. Tall tales of Paul Bunyan's feats alongside his sidekick Babe, the Blue Ox, originated with North American loggers and was then popularized in a 1916 promotional pamphlet for the Red River Lumber Company. He is usually portrayed with a black beard and wearing a red plaid shirt with his blue ox friend.

Pennsylvania Station (1910–)

Also known as Penn Station, it is the main

railroad station in New York City where people would connect with intercity trains and those leaving the city. It was serving 600,000 passengers per day as of 2019. To go home, Mona would disembark in Cincinnati at the Union Terminal Station to board another train going to Lexington, Ky. However, she would not go through Cincinnati to get to Montana leaving from Penn Station—most probably she would make a connection at Chicago going west. Don't confuse NYC Grand Central Station with NYC Penn Station.

Pinkerton National Detective Agency (1850s—)

The Pinkertons is a private security firm created by Allan Pinkerton in the 1850s. The agency performed services ranging from security guarding to private military work. At the height of their power, they were hired by wealthy businessmen to infiltrate unions and intimidate workers. During the Homestead Strike of 1892, the Pinkertons confronted striking steel workers, causing the death of three Pinkertons and nine workers. The Pinkerton Agency is now a division of a Swedish company—Securitas AB.

Shangri-La

Shangri-La is the name of a mythical valley in the 1933 novel *Lost Horizon* by James Hilton. The name has become synonymous with a place of refuge where the inhabitants live long lives without strife—an earthly paradise. President Franklin D. Roosevelt renamed the 125 acre WPA presidential retreat, originally known as Hi-Catoctin, to Shangri-La in 1942. President Eisenhower renamed Shangri-La to Camp David in 1953 to honor his father and grandson, both named David.

Sixes and Sevens

Slang for disorganization or a difficult situation.

Snyder Act

It wasn't until 1924, four years after the 19th Amendment allowing women to vote, that Native Americans were declared U.S. citizens and given the full right to vote under the Snyder Act. Still, many Native Americans were prevented from voting as the Constitution left it up to the states to decide who may vote. It took forty years for fifty states to comply, even though Native Americans were paying U.S. taxes and were legally bound to U.S. laws.

Swells

A 1930s slang term to describe people of wealth and privilege used in a derogatory way.

Trousers/Slacks

In the late 19th and early 20th century, women, riding bikes and enjoying other athletic activities, adopted a form of pants called bloomers or knickerbockers. During WWI, women, working in factories and citing safety as a concern, threw off their dresses and wore pants but it was socially frowned upon. Three women were mainly responsible for American women wearing pants in the 1930s. German actress Marlene Dietrich's character in the 1930 film *Morocco*, was considered scandalous as she dressed in a tux and kissed a female audience member on the lips. First Lady, Eleanor Roosevelt wore trousers at the White House Easter Egg Roll in 1933. The woman who had the most influence on women wearing trousers was American actress Katharine Hepburn, who was the first woman to wear pants in a motion picture and was photographed wearing them in her private life. Wearing pants became socially acceptable when Rosie the Riveter, the iconic symbol of American women working in factories supporting the WWII effort, wore pants in her famous cover of the *Saturday Evening Post*.

White Collar Workers

Upton Sinclair, an American author, coined the term in the 1930s referring to clerical and administrative workers. Men, who worked in managerial positions, usually wore white, starched shirts with collars to work.

William Donovan (1883–1959)

Donovan was an American soldier, lawyer, and intelligence officer. Donovan is the only veteran to receive all four of the United States highest awards—the Medal of Honor, the Distinguished Service Cross, the Distinguished Service Medal, and the National Security Medal plus the Silver Star and the Purple Heart. He is best known for serving as the head of the Office of Strategic Services (OSS) during WWII. Another famous alumnus of the OSS was French gourmet chef, Julia Child. The OSS evolved to become the Central Intelligence Agency (CIA) after 1945. Donovan was recruited by President Roosevelt in 1934 to "casually" collect information against

Nazi sympathizers living in the U.S. as the States did not have a formal protocol as spying was frowned upon. Secretary of State Henry L. Stimson, under President Hoover, wrote in his memoirs, "Gentlemen do not read each other's mail," and pulled funding for intelligence gathering. Roosevelt knew that Donovan was a loud critic of such action and felt the U.S. needed a formal intelligence department like the United Kingdom's MI5 and MI6. As soon as the U.S. was attacked in 1941, Roosevelt demanded that he be granted money for such a department with Donovan heading it. Thus began the OSS. Years later, Donovan died after acquiring dementia, taking all his secrets with him to the grave. A statue of Donovan stands in the CIA Headquarters lobby.

Wobblies (1905–)

They are members of the Industrial Workers of the World (IWW) which was a radical labor union formed in 1905. They were an alternative to the American Federation of Labor (AFL), which had closed membership to those who were not white males. The IWW wanted to open membership to all laborers. IWW is closely associated with communism and used violence, sabotage, and strikes to make change. The IWW now works within the law to effect social change.

Murder Under A Honey Moon

Mona Moon and her new husband, Robert Farley, Duke of Brynelleth are on their honeymoon at last. They have just boarded the SS City of Paris ocean liner. The couple are looking forward to visiting Robert's ancestral English home, Brynelleth, and then off to Paris before winding up their honeymoon on the Italian Rivera. After a romantic evening of champagne and dancing until the wee hours of the night, Mona and Robert discover their suite has been ransacked and Mona's jewelry supposedly secured in the purser's office has been stolen.

Mona is horrified as some of the jewelry belongs to the Brynelleth Estate and were cherished pieces of Robert's mother. The ocean liner is searched by the ship's crew, and a diamond tiara turns up in a bartender's cabin. It is the same bartender who served Mona and Robert earlier in the evening. The only problem is the bartender has been murdered and the rest of the jewelry is still missing.

Other Books By Abigail Keam

Mona Moon Mysteries

Josiah Reynolds Mysteries

About The Author

Abigail Keam is an award-winning and international best-selling author. She is a beekeeper, loves chocolate, and lives on a cliff overlooking the Kentucky River. Besides the 1930s Mona Moon Mysteries, she writes the award-winning *Josiah Reynolds Mysteries*, *The Princess Maura Tales* (fantasy) and the *Last Chance For Love Series* (sweet romance).

Don't forget to leave a review! Tell your friends about Mona.

Thank you again, gentle reader, for your reviews and your word of mouth, which are so important for any book. I hope to meet you again between the pages.